Donn Piatt

The lone Grave of the Shenandoah

And other Tales

Donn Piatt

The lone Grave of the Shenandoah
And other Tales

ISBN/EAN: 9783743341968

Manufactured in Europe, USA, Canada, Australia, Japa

Cover: Foto ©Andreas Hilbeck / pixelio.de

Manufactured and distributed by brebook publishing software (www.brebook.com)

Donn Piatt

The lone Grave of the Shenandoah

THE LONE GRAVE OF THE SHENANDOAH

THE

LONE GRAVE OF THE SHENANDOAH

AND OTHER TALES

BY DONN PIATT

BELFORD, CLARKE & CO.
CHICAGO, NEW YORK. AND SAN FRANCISCO
1888

To My Wife.

THE BLOOM WAS ON THE ALDER AND THE TASSEL ON THE CORN.

I HEARD the bob-white whistle in the dewy breath of morn;
The bloom was on the alder and the tassel on the corn.
I stood with beating heart beside the babbling Mac o-chee,
To see my love come down the glen to keep her tryst with me.

I saw her pace, with quiet grace, the shaded path along,
And pause to pluck a flower, or hear the thrush's song.
Denied by her proud father as a suitor to be seen,
She came to me, with loving trust, my gracious little queen.

Above my station, Heaven knows, that gentle maiden shone,
For she was belle and wide beloved, and I a youth unknown,
The rich and great about her thronged, and sought on bended knee
For love this gracious princess gave with all her heart to me.

So, like a startled fawn, before my longing eyes she stood,
With all the freshness of a girl in flush of womanhood.
I trembled as I put my arm about her form divine,
And stammered as, in awkward speech, I begged her to be mine.

'Tis sweet to hear the pattering rain that lulls a dim-lit dream;
'Tis sweet to hear the song of birds, and sweet the rippling stream;
'Tis sweet amid the mountain pines to hear the south winds sigh—
More sweet than these and all besides was th' loving, low reply.

The little hand I held in mine held all I had of life,
To mould its better destiny and soothe to sleep its strife.
'Tis said that angels watch o'er men, commissioned from above;
My angel walked with me on earth and gave to me her love.

Ah! dearest wife, my heart is stirred, my eyes are dim with tears;
I think upon the loving faith of all these bygone years:
For now we stand upon this spot, as in that dewy morn,
With the bloom upon the alder and the tassel on the corn.

CONTENTS.

vi   *CONTENTS.*

NOVEL VIII.

PREFACE.

THE tales of love and labor collected in this little volume had their origin in an attempt to respond to a long-felt want in the pocketbook of their author. That they failed to fill that aching void--the vacuum which nature, human nature abhors--was not owing so much to a lack of excellence in the book itself as to the law of supply and demand, which is about the only law vouchsafed our American author. Lacking any other law, especially one granting an international copyright, theft augments the supply and gluts the market of demand. Eminently respectable publishers—respectable because rich—and a pensive public have been content, the one to enjoy and the other to fatten on stolen goods.

A number of earnest fanatics were hanged at Chicago for holding that all property is theft, and resisting with bombs a police with pistols that joined issue with them on this proposition. The majesty of the law was maintained under the gallows, and the axiom established that all property is held under a sacred right sanctioned by God and sustained by common law and written constitutions, save and except that form of human industry called a book. A man may work his idea into a sewing machine, for example, and the courts will punish by imprisonment any anarchist or communist who dares appropriate the machine. But if he work his idea into a book, it is a common possession, and may be appropriated by any anarchist disguised as a publisher, and enjoyed by the public without compensation. If a misguided son of man approach the sewing-machine for the purpose of taking and carrying off the same, the proprietor may use bombs in its defence, and public opinion, that is law, will approve of the defence. This, however, does not extend to the author of a book, and as such he must submit patiently to the spoliation.

For nearly a century the authors of the United States have been knocking in a feeble manner at the bronze doors of Congress in search of a remedy for this wrong. From time to time the doors have been opened, but the result is invariably defeat. This comes mainly from the fact that Congress is a political body, with no literary or scientific s de, and the authors are scientific or literary, with no knowledge of or taste for politics. No Congressman ever reads a book. He would not be a Congressman if he did. No scientific or literary man studies or cares for politics. The result is that the two august bodies are strangers to each other ; and the condition is not improved by an intr duction. A distinguished Senator, the late President Lincoln's prominent rival for a nominat on at Chica o, gave our authors a name that clings to them yet about Washington, as " them literary fellers; " and the book compilers are not slow to retaliate upon the Solons as " vile politicians."

The writer of this sat for ten years in the reporters' galleries of Congress, and in that time learned to know the body of so-called law makers, which a witty correspondent designated as " the delegated stupidity " of the United States. Whether this is correct or not, the writer saw in the House the "cave of the winds," and in the Senate a dead " fog-bank." which had long since ceased to be lifted by the thunders of a Webster or lit by the lightning of a Calhoun

This observant reporter was taught that Congress never legislated designedly upon any subject other than that found in providing ways and means to carry on the Government. Left to itself, the one constitutional duty was to meet, pass the appropriation bills, and adjourn.

Lying back of the grave body, and not by any means concealed, is a power that prompts legislation and passes laws. This third house, and master of both houses, is the lobby. The lobby is to Congress what a bar is to a court. It is composed of the accredited agents of our legislative branch of the Government, and is a necessity. Since the war the General Government has entered the field of private enterprise, and under pretext of encouraging capital and protecting labor, seeks to insure a profit to certain moneyed interests. As the Government has no means of its own to pay these bounties, it gains its end in that direction by taxation. That is, the tax is so adjusted that for every cent collected to sustain the Government, three cents are assessed to pay the pet interests. We rob Peter to recompense Paul, and as Peter represents a vast majority of consumers, the process is extremely cheerful to all concerned.

This fetches to the capital vast crowds of people interested in securing this bounty from the Government. Said General Schenck, chairman of the Committee on Ways and Means, when apologizing for his late appearance at a breakfast given him : " I was routed out of bed by an anti-cow-kicker, and chased in here by grindstones, india-rubber goods, and hoop-skirts." Every possible interest and business is represented at Washington save that of labor and agriculture.

Now, all legislation is done by Congress through committees. A member introduces a bill and it is referred to its appropriate committee. The Lycurgus sees it disappear through a door into a room where the committee sits twice a week from ten A.M. till twelve noon. He may follow his bill to this secret and extremely irritable body, but he seldom does. He is too busy for that His entire time from the rising of the sun to the setting thereof is given to attending to the wants of his constituents. His mails come loaded with letters demanding attention to everything on earth but the purpose for which he was elected. If he neglects these to study legislation, he is doomed. He will not be re-elected.

The parties thus interested in legislation must seek the accredited agents of Congress, called the lobby, to attend to their business. Those selected by Congress are made up mainly of fast men and loose women. The same corps, selected for the same purpose, about any legislative body of Europe is composed of learned and respectable men. Our Congress will have none of that. " Nous avons changé tout cela." And Congress has so far succeeded in securing its agents of the lobby, that it is ruir. to the character of any reputable man to be seen in their midst. Efforts have been made, from time to time, to purify this body, but ever in vain. The representation represents. and the fountain never rises above its head When Richard B. Irwin said to the Pacific Mail Company that if it would employ the accredited agent of Congress called the lobby, and pay it a million of dollars, the sought-for subsidy would be obtained—and so it was—Mr. Irwin was cruelly abused; but no one paused to consider the condition of a Congress that demonstrated the truth of his assertion.

As a member of the Authors' League, the writer of this undertook to enlighten the book-makers as to the real condition at the capital. He was treated with lofty contempt. The poets, novelists, scientific delvers, and other bookworms went up to the Capitol to plead the justice of their demand.

There is nothing that exasperates a member so much as to have his time occupied by a consideration of the merits of a measure—unless the measure is political, and directly or indirectly affects his return to office. The bearer of such meritorious measure not political is a bore. The member shuts and double-locks his door. If he sees his enemy on the street he incontinently dives down a back alley. Getting his card upon the floor, he hides in the cloak-room and blasphemes. The advocate of such meritorious measure is a crank and a nuisance.

The lobby understands this and eschews the merit. He bases his claim on its p litical aspect, which means immediate good to the law-maker.

The maker of books cannot be taught any of this. He knows all about it. His conceit is only equalled by his profound ignorance, for he is college-bred and literary trained. He says truly with Southey:

> My days among the dead are passed,
>   Around me I behold,
> Where'er these casual eyes are cast,
>   The mighty minds of old.

The living alone are dead and unknown to him. The great world goes roaring on around him, dimly heard and dimly seen through the loophole of his book-lined vault, wherein rest his mighty dead of a half-forgotten past. Books built on books are of no good. Yet such is his work. The departed whose bones he worships were men among men. He is like the artist who studies great masters and sits a little fellow on a step-ladder, copying, instead of facing nature, and getting his inspiration from whence the masters won their immortality.

How little science and literature move and affect humanity one may learn from a few facts. These facts teach us that all the great discoveries and inventions that subvert the law of the material world to man's use were made mainly by ignorant men who stumbled upon them. As for literature, it is the merest trifle. Let us see We have a population of sixty odd millions in these United States. Of these it is a liberal estimate to say that three milli ns read books. Of the three millions the larger part read love stories, mostly trash. Small wonder the politicians designate authors as " literary fellers " of small account. Yet, when one of these puts himself between the covers of a book, and secures a sale of a thousand copies, he swells in his own estimation to an object of much public interest, and designs a monument.

Their latest eff rt before Congress was simply pitiable. They appeared at Washington and gave public readings, through which to raise funds, not to employ the lobby or subsidize the press, but to pay their board-bills. But for James Whitcomb Riley and Mark Twain, with their grotesque humor, the shows would have been dismal failures. The wives and daughters of a few millionaire Senators bought tickets, and the wealthy people of Washington yawned dismally in their seats until Whitcomb Riley, a man of genius, who got his inspiration from living men while painting signs for country stores, came to the rescue.

In the committee-room the poor fellows met their masters, the publishers who have grown fat on theft, and then encountered their terrible foe, the sixty thousand printers of the Typographical Union. Our authors dropped into a mild condition that lost all the indignation against unquestionable iniquity. A compromise was agreed on that, like all compromises with sin, strengthens the evil. Better half a loaf than no bread, said one, with an eager concurrence on the part of all. Poor fellows ! There was not one of them, save Mark Twain, who was not dependent on these same thriving publishers for their daily crust. They did not get their half loaf. They asked for bread and got a stone. The bill provides that the foreign author may have a right to his property provided the American pirate shall consent to the enjoyment. That is, it is stipulated that if within a given time the foreign author shall find favor with an American publisher to reproduce his book, his right shall be recognized ; but failing in this he can be plundered as of old.   In other words, the right is made dependent on the will of the thieves, and they can make such terms as they please ; or in other words, a legalized fraud.

What poor stuff is this! And yet these kings of thought marched out as if they had accomplished a great victory.

Strange to say, that through all this contention, nearly a century old, there exists all the right of property for which King Higginson and King Howells and other potentates of the pen have so earnestly striven.   Some twelve years since Mr. Lewis Abrams, of Washington, a thoughtful man and a hard student, came to the front with a legal opinion on the subject that is conclusive as to the right of the foreign author to his property in the United States.   He called attention to the fact that a book had a commercial side to it other than its scientific or literary value.   This, under the common law of trade, since recognized by t eatics, secures a property right in any manufactured article, be it a book or book-muslin, that can be sold.   To protect this a trade mark is recognized, and all the civilized world has resolved that the trademark shall be held sacred.   When, therefore, an author files the title-page of his forthcoming work with the Librarian of Congress, he gets in return a copyright that is in fact a trade-mark. Under our treaties, the highest law of the land, this trade-mark is as good for a book as it is for balbriggan hose or a peculiar make of Scotch tweed.   What more do you want, oh Higginson, Howells, and other " kings of thought "

> " Who wage contention with their time's decay,
>   And of the past are all that will not pass away " ?

"A race of shopkeepers makes a nation of thieves," said the gr at Napoleon; but even a nation of thieves respect the trade mark.

Donn Piatt,

Mac-o-chee, Ohio, March 29, 1888.

THE LONE GRAVE OF THE SHENANDOAH.

NOVEL I.

THE old stone tavern known through generations as the Indian Queen, that stands on a turn of the road down the mountains from Sherryville to M—— , of the Shenandoah Valley, enjoys a landscape a castle might be proud of. That this is the Indian Queen runs on tradition and general consent, for the old-fashioned signboard that creaks in front lost long since the work of art that pictured forth the name. Nothing remained on the one side but a dim crown of feathers, nearly obliterated, and two staring eyes on the other, that, put together by the curious observer, failed to make up that imaginary creature known to tradition and dime novels as Her Majesty Queen Pocahontas.

Virginia's little romance of that ilk is about as dim as the signboard. Pocahontas did live and was the daughter of a chief. But all else is the fringe-work of fancy, that, like the sign, would have long since faded out but for a useful purpose the romance serves, and that is, the manner in which our loved ancestors had of accounting for—well, say brunettes that appeared from time to time among the noble Virginians.

To return, however, to my story : The view from the rude porch of the inn is exceedingly beautiful, for it contains one of the loveliest portions of that lovely valley. The green meadows and rich fields, with groves and gleams of water, dotted by white farm-houses half hid in orchards, were all framed in by mountains, the summits of which seemed to melt into the blue of heaven, leaving the eye in doubt as to where the rounded rocky or wooded tops ended and the clouds began. The sulphury smoke of battle had obscured these fields, and the mountains had echoed back the mouthing cannon of combatants, but at the time our little romance opens no harm had been done to the valley itself. Armies had marched, fought, and retreated—generally, up to that time, the dear old flag had hurried ingloriously out of the row—but no great injury had come to the work of the farmer or the beauty of nature.

The summer sun was sinking in the hazy west, with distant rumblings of artillery telling of a far-off combat, as a girl, some twenty years of age, sat in a rocking-chair, on the wooden porch of the tavern, rocking softly to and fro, and gazing dreamily upon the view before her. Her appearance was such as to attract attention. In dress, bearing, and expression there was a refinement that indicated one city bred, rather than of rural local origin. She was exceedingly attractive, with a claim to beauty that came under the head of handsome rather that pretty. Her face, at rest, indicated more force of character than that which ordinarily falls to the sweeter sex. The perfect oval ended in a pronounced chin, while the slight aquiline line of her nose made that chin aggressive. But for the full red lips of the perfect mouth, and large dreamy eyes, the pale face would have been too severe to excite other that a feeling of admiration.

The expression depicted from time to time, as the feelings changed, had a wider range than is usual to such a cast of countenance. As her eyes wandered over the beautiful view her face was one to admire. When a little three-year-old daughter of the stone tavern toddled to her and rested its little head upon her knee, the long silken fringes of her tender eyes fell upon it as her slender hands stroked its curly locks—and her face was one to love. Afterward, when she gazed at the brigade of Union soldiers pitching their tents on the meadows below, scorn and hate gave her a face to fear.

A movement below made her start, as if to leave her chair. Then, after half rising, she settled back and began again the monotonous rocking. A cavalcade of officers was riding up the road, as if coming to the Indian Queen.

At the head of this little escort rode a stout, middle-aged gentleman, in the uniform of a Brigadier General of the Northern Army. Mounted on a superb horse, he sat with the ease of an experienced rider, his high rounded shoulders holding a grim, resolute head, that under other than a military hat would have been repulsive in its severity.   There was a face not to be trifled with, as the historic annals of war and diplomacy have put to record.

Halting in front of the tavern, the officers dismounted, and as the orderlies led the horses to the stable, they ascended the steps, and gaining the porch instinctively lifted their hats to the girl before them.   She barely recognized the salutation, then continued her rocking, as if their politeness and presence were alike indifferent to her.

A grim change in the General's face left one in doubt whether he was suffering from a toothache or indulging in a smile.

On the landlord making his appearance the chief gave his orders.   They were for supper for himself and staff, one room for the night, and quarters for a corporal's guard.   While the supper was being prepared the General sat in the split-bottomed arm-chair, near our heroine. while the members of his staff, weary of a long day's ride, stretched themselves upon the sod under the trees.

> "How many a vanished hour and day
> Have sunlight o'er me shed "

since last I parted from that gallant band of good fellows a loved General held together during the four years of a terrible conflict. I can see them now.   I see the tall, slender, volatile Chestnutt, gay as a lark, brave as a lion.   Esterhaze, quiet, grave, yet ever alert to duty.   Comb, slender and awkward, but possessed of the keenest sense of humor, as ready to jest under fire as in the camp.   Then came old Grenville, called old because he was so solemn.   It would take a surgical instrument to get a joke in his head, and then another to get it out.   And last, but not least, for he is the hero of my little romance, Bob Ellersly, young, handsome, and liable to love and debt.

Two of these met violent deaths, and the rest are scattered world-wide apart.   I send them greeting.

"I say, Bob," cried Chestnutt to the aide, as he rested his head on his elbows and kicked his toes into the grass, "rather handsome girl that up there."

"The old man seems to have discovered that," Bob responded. "See him doing the sweet on her, will you?"

"Well, he is," Comb chipped in, "but he isn't making much headway, I gather, from the expression on her lovely countenance."

The General was doing the suave polite, for which he was famous, and getting little in return but crisp monosyllables.

It does not require much time to prepare a meal in Virginia. Ham and eggs, with hot biscuits, make the substantials, while sticky, indigestible sweets, called preserves, form the entrées. The General and staff were soon called to table, and ate with the hearty relish of hungry men. After the supper had been disposed of the General called his aide, Bob Ellersly, to one side and said :

"I have a rather pleasant duty for you, Bob."

"All right, General, the pleasanter the better."

"It is one, Lieutenant," continued the commander, "of extreme delicacy, and I trust to your tact to carry it to a successful issue. Now, don't let any of your boyish impulses make you blunder. You see that young lady on the porch?"

"I believe I noticed her."

"Well, for the next ten days, or until further orders, you must not permit her to get out of your sight. You must do this delicately, for she is the niece of the most prominent and important loyalist of Baltimore. It will not do to offend her, for the whole affair may be a mistake after all."

"What is the affair, General?"

"Simply this : the Secretary of War writes me that all the papers concerning the coming campaign in Virginia were stolen from the department and traced to Clara Willis, of Baltimore. Miss Clara has since disappeared, but there is every reason to believe that she is somewhere in the Shenandoah Valley trying to communicate with the enemy. This is the girl, Bob, I am satisfied. I worried enough out of the landlord to convince me I am right Put a guard about the house so no one can enter or leave without your permission, and keep your eye on her."

"But, General, this is difficult. If I am not to make her a prisoner, how am I to act?"

"Make love to her, Bob," said his commander, with a twinkle

in his eye. "Sacrifice yourself on the altar of your country. She is a woman, and a devilish pretty one, and, therefore, may be wooed ; she is a woman and, therefore, may be won." So saying the Brigadier ordered horses. and Bob heard them rattling off in the moonlight, leaving him to execute his diplomatic mission.

Calling Corporal Bang, Bob directed him to place a guard in front of the house, and another in the rear, with orders to permit no one to enter or leave, man, woman, or child, without his (the Lieutenant's) orders.

"Do you know, Corporal, what has become of the young lady who was seated on the porch before supper?"

"She skooted up-stairs, Lieutenant, and every swish of her petticoats had a secesh cuss in it. She lit up the corner room, I calculate."

"Very well, you have your orders."

"All right, Lieutenant."

Bob Ellersly seated himself in the vacated arm-chair and smoked his briar-wood pipe in the moonlight, revolving over and over in his mind the strange duty imposed upon him. He was interested, and yet did not like the business. Young, ardent, and ambitious, he thought of his comrades riding off to glory, while he remained behind to circumvent a woman. Bouncing from his chair, he walked the rough boards of the old porch impatiently. Suddenly he descended the steps and stood under the trees, gazing up at that corner of the room occupied by the enemy. Country taverns are not graced with curtains, but something of the sort had been improvised for this apartment, and he could only see a shadow of the inmate, passing and repassing, as if she, too, was restless and impatient.

As he stood leaning against a tree in the moonlight he presented as handsome a figure as one would care to see. The broad shoulders, swung over slender hips, held over them a head in which youth and manhood contended for the mastery. His face was boyish when at rest, but when animated he seemed to take on years in the way of expression which, added to his soldierly bearing, impressed his comrades as one capable of any duty. Left an orphan at an early age, with a small property, on which he had been educated, he stood alone in the world. He had not, he said, a relation that he knew of on earth. "So much the better," grunted cynical Comb, "if you have poor relations you fear they will want to borrow your money, or get hung ; if you have rich ones they are sure to get into Congress, or the penitentiary, and worry the life out of you. Relations are nuisances."

The next morning Ellersly informed Bang in the presence of the landlord that they had been left to look after the forwarding of important despatches from the front, and with an orderly rode to Murrayville. He was scarcely out of sight before an ancient gig, that wabbled in the wheels and groaned in the body, as if afflicted with combined old age and sciatica, was drawn in front by an animated hat-rack for a horse. The negro driver stopped at the foot of the steps, and our heroine, fully prepared for a jaunt, seated herself by the colored boy. When the horse was turned toward the road the private on guard brought his musket down before the horse's nose and arrested the concern.

"What's the meaning of this?" demanded the girl.

"Can't go, that's all."

" Call your corporal ; I want to know the meaning of this outrage."

Corporal Bang stepped to the front.

"What is the reason for this detention?" she continued.

"Them as gives orders has reasons ; them as gets orders has bayonets," sententiously responded Bang.

There was no help for it. With flushed cheeks and a firm, set mouth, the girl descended from the vehicle and entered the house. Every step was a protest. The ancient gig was restored to its *maison de santé* and the hat-rack of a horse to its stall. At noon Ellersly returned, and learned of the attempted escape. After dinner, while smoking his pipe, the suspected girl approached him.

" I attempted to drive out this morning, sir," she said indignantly, "and was arrested by your men. Am I to understand that I am a prisoner?"

"I am very sorry, madam," answered the aide, avoiding the question, "very sorry so rude a thing was done."

"Don't apologize, sir. We know your miserable Government makes war on women. You are only a hireling executing its brutal orders. Again I ask you, am I a prisoner?"

"It is really painful to know that you entertain such an idea," patiently continued the officer. "These men execute orders so literally that mistakes like this will occur."

"I am not a prisoner, then?"

"You are at liberty, I assure you, to go where and when you please. To prove to you, however, how unjust you are to us I will add that you shall go as you will and owing to the unsettled and dangerous condition the country is in, I will furnish you an escort of armed men to see that you go in safety."

"Mr. Lieutenant," she said with scorn, "when I need your services, I will ask them."

"Do so, madam, and you will find me ready to serve you." And so they parted.

"An unpleasant beginning for a love affair," murmured Bob, resuming his pipe.

For the next twenty-four hours the Lieutenant saw little of his suspect, and the little he did see was not agreeable. Meeting her by accident on the stairs she not only gave way, but gathered her skirts about her, as if she feared contamination from the touch.

The day after, however, her mood changed. She received him with a bewitching smile, holding out her little hand, saying :

"Mr. ——" and she paused.

"Ellersly," he added, lifting his cap.

"Mr. Ellersly, I wish to apologize for my rude talk. I forgot that you were an officer on duty, and what is more, I forgot that I was a lady. Pardon me."

"I have no pardon to grant, madam," said Bob, gallantly. "Reproof is sweeter from some than commendation from others. Now, what can I do for you?"

"We will breakfast together," she said, "and then I will tell you."

At breakfast she poured out his muddy coffee of beans and chiccory, and was so very amiable that Bob, young as he was, could not help thinking she was too confoundedly sweet, and he became, in consequence. the more alert and suspicious.

"Now I'll tell you, Lieutenant," she said on the porch, "I am ashamed to confess it, but I have some poor relations in these mountains almost starved by the war."

"That is a lie," thought Bob, but he said nothing—only smiled sweetly.

"I wish to communicate with and help them," she continued, "and if you will furnish me with an escort I will make the attempt."

An ambush, thought Bob; but he smiled all the more and added :

"Why, of course I will.   I'll do better—I will be your escort myself.   Shall we go immediately?"

"Oh, no, there is no need of such haste ; to-morrow will do," and they dropped into conversation as natural as if they knew each other for years.   Bob was shrewd, but inexperienced.   He did not observe the dangerous thread of the talk.   While dexterously avoiding all reference to herself she kept on that most fascinating subject to all men, when guided by a pretty woman—himself.   It was Othello and Desdemona over again.   Only Desdemona led the conversation.   Ah, me, if the beguiling sex only knew the full power in their little ears, aided by deep, earnest eyes, none of us would be safe.   Bob talked well, at times eloquently, with a golden thread of humor running through all, and he who set out to deceive through love-making went to his bed deep in love with the fair charmer.

The day after the expedition was attempted.   Alas ! it proved a miserable failure.   The old horse pulled them slowly to the summit of the mountain, and then descending to the valley beyond stumbled at every step, and at last fell down, breaking the shaft, and throwing the fair emissary on his phrenological rump.

When a horse falls he takes a philosophical view of the situation and lies still.   Old Smooth Tooth lay stretched upon the road, whith his shoeless hoofs full extended and his eyes half closed, as if to say, "This is the end ; farewell, vain world ; leave me to the buzzards."

Ellersly lifted his fair companion from the embrace of the moist anatomy. She got up laughing merrily over the mishap, and, leaving the wreck to the man, the two walked back.

"This is too bad," said Bob. "The poor relations will never get relief at this rate. Look here, Miss Clara"—he had her name—"can you ride?"

"Like an Arab," she responded.

"Good!" he exclaimed. "Now, if I can find a saddle, you shall have my horse Chancellor. He is splendid. I will ride one of the orderly's horses, and so we will penetrate every recess of the mountains."

She was delighted with the arrangement, and an old-fashioned single-horned side-saddle, hard as the rock of ages, was fished out from the stables. Bob worked long and laboriously in fashioning one of his best blankets to the old affair, to make it more presentable as well as easier, and the rides began.

Chancellor, when first mounted, snorted, reared, and lunged, as if indignant, but the fair girl kept her seat composedly until the steed quieted down, and then patting his arched neck put herself on friendly terms with the noble animal.

Those rides were long and frequent. Both enjoyed them. She was sweetly confidential in her young escort's life and affairs, and every hour the delicious chain of love bound the poor boy nearer and firmer to his adoration. Small wonder. The young girl was simply superb on horseback. The close-fitting riding dress seemed part of her supple, graceful, engaging form, while the exercise and excitement brought a delicate, shell-tinted rosiness to her cheeks, that seemed the one thing necessary to make her pale face perfect. Bob longed to avow his love, but youth is timid when the precious treasure may be jeopardized by the avowal. He was blinded by his passion, and did not see the game so openly played by the little gambler. She was a true daughter of the South, and her heart was with her poor brothers marching shoeless, with scant raiment, poorly armed, sleeping without shelter, and dying by thousands with desperate bravery for their cause. To have that in her possession that was, as she believed, of vital importance to them, made her desperate. For such a cause she would play the Judith, and had

Bob avowed his love, she was resolved to accept, let the consequences have been what they might to the poor lad.

Oh ! the golden glory of those sunny days. They took on a roseate hue, that made the blue summits of the mountains a deeper blue, as if to bound that Eden that lies about each life in the golden glow of youth, when love touches the sweet, tender existence, and the birds sing, and the flowers bloom with voices and odors that penetrate the very soul, never again to pass away. The scene fades, the birds die, and the flowers perish, oft in the hard realities of life the blue mountains no longer frame in the fairy paradise, but all the same we cling to it through existence, as our first parents clung to the Garden to which they never could return.

Shakespeare tells us the course of true love never does run smooth. No, indeed ; life's ways are not fitted for the sweet stream. For a little while it murmurs along green meadows, and then, anon, it falls among rocks and rough ways, and oftentimes is dashed over precipices to be dissipated in thin mist, over which arches the rainbow, not, alas ! of hope, but memory.

There were some little tricks the lovely girl indulged in that exasperated her lover, who, although blinded by his passion, had not lost sight of his duty. One of these was to stop at some mountain hut, and persist in dismounting and entering the hovel. Bob dismounted also, and would help her to the ground and accompany her to the interior. He kept his eyes and ears alert, and believed that he baffled any designs in this direction.

Another fancy indulged in was to banter the Lieutenant to a race and dart off on Chancellor, at the best of his running pace, and Bob, on his Government horse, would follow lumbering after, scarce keeping her in sight, until it suited the girl to check up. Bob remonstrated in vain, and all he could do was to direct the orderly to keep a sharp lookout on either side of the road for anything the girl might drop.

One day Corporal Bang, who happened to be the escort, handed the Lieutenant a letter, tied to a stone, that he had picked up from a gully after one of these races.

"Got a reminder through my chappo, Lieutenant, when I picked that up," and he showed a hole in his hat.

Ellersly looked longingly at the missive. It was directed to a well-known guerilla of the mountains. Bob would have given a good deal to know its contents. But he quietly handed it, without a word, to the girl. Her face flushed, and somewhat embarrassed she hurried to her room. In a few minutes, however, she returned, letter in hand, with her cheeks yet holding the flush of her excitement.

"Lieutenant Ellersly," she asked, in an even, steady tone, that was forced, "why did you not open this letter?"

"Open your letter?" he asked in turn.

"Yes, open my letter. You are not doing your duty to your Government."

"Miss Clara." said the boy proudly. "I tendered my life to my country. I did not include in that my honor. When I am sunk so low as to steal, I cease to be worthy of my commission."

The girl tore open the letter. "Then!" she cried, "learn who I am, and what I am trying to do."

He took the letter and deliberately tore it into fragments, throwing the bits to the wind from the porch. "Miss Clara," he exclaimed excitedly, "I know all I want to know of you. You are doing your duty, as you see it, like a brave hearted woman, for your side; leave me to do mine, as a gentleman, for mine."

She looked at him earnestly, half in surprise and half in tenderness, and said in an undertone, as if speaking to herself, "My task grows harder than I thought for." Then she added, offering her hand, "Let us be as kind to each other as we can."

The day after this strange interview she insisted upon their daily ride, although the morn opened with a thunder-storm, and the rain came down at intervals in torrents. Ellersly remonstrated, but she laughed, saying. "We are soldiers, you know, and must not be cowed by a little rain."

They started, followed by Corporal Bang, and after an hour's riding gained the summit of the mountain, along which the road ran for a mile or more comparatively level, and then she cried: "Now for my last race," and started on the run. Bob followed as well as he could, and while lumbering along, the girl rapidly gaining upon him, he remembered that at the end of a mile the road sloped down gradually to the river, and he also remembered a gully, along which ran a path dangerous for a horse, but that cut off half the distance to the point where the main road touched the stream. Instinctively he plunged down the deep declivity. Fortunately his horse, though slow, was sure-footed, and in a few minutes he gained the bank. He gained this just in time to see his fair fugitive enter a light boat and push into the stream. He was below the point she debarked, and saw before she could get hold of the oars that the boat, caught in the swift stream, was floating down to where a large tree, nearly level with the water, leaned over the stream. She would pass under this, and running out he swung down, catching a limb with his knee, and caught the skiff with his right hand. At that instant the sharp crack of a rifle rung out from the opposite shore, and Bob fell wounded into the boat.

His weight nearly upset the frail craft, but it righted, whirled around, and the next instant the girl pulled it to the shore. Leaping to the bank she beached the boat half its length, and then reaching to him said :

" Are you much hurt ? "

" I believe so," he answered, as, half crawling, he worked his way out and fell upon the ground. A second shot from the same quarter struck the ground within an inch of his body.

" The cowardly miscreant," she said, throwing herself upon him. "If he kills you, he must kill me."

Poor Bob gave a grateful look and a weak smile in return for this act of devotion. At that instant the clatter of a horse's hoofs were heard upon the pike. Corporal Bang appeared. Taking in the situation at a glance, he dismounted, pushed the girl one side, and picking up Ellersly as he would a child, carried him round the bend of the road, that made a shelter from further shots. Placing the Lieutenant timidly upon the grass he asked :

" Are you hit bad, Lieutenant ? "

" Bad enough, Corporal, he gasped, and then added, " water."

Clara started hurriedly to the river. As she appoached the brink she took the beautiful little leather sack Bob had so often eyed suspiciously from her belt, opened it, drew out a package of papers, threw them into the stream, and then, stooping, filled the sack with water. When she returned Bang was cutting the blouse from the boy's shoulder, exhibiting a wound not larger than a pea, from which the blood spurted like a fountain. At the sight the girl nearly fainted, but rallying, administered the draught to his eager lips.

Again the girl hurried away. Throwing off her riding-dress she took her linen underskirt, tore it into strips, and, without waiting to put on her dress, handed them to Bang, and then assisted him in binding up the wound. She presented a strange sight to the two men in her short skirt, for the collar and linen cover were displaced, and the white column of neck and snowy precipice of shoulder were exposed. She did not seem to be aware of her exposure, and started, blushing crimson, when Bang said :

"Now, Miss, git on your toggery and sit here while I go for an ambulance. Give him a sip of this times along," he continued, handing her his canteen that seemed full of commissary whiskey. Catching Chancellor, as the best horse of the three, he mounted, without waiting to change saddles, and rode off at a gallop.

The girl, once more in her riding-habit, seated herself, and putting her arms about the wounded man drew his head upon her shoulder, like a little mother, all care and tenderness. The storm had passed, the sun came out above the mountains, warm and bright, and the mocking-bird, in the cedars near, poured out its flood of joyous melody. The poor boy's passion found utterance at last, and in words made eloquent by gasps and pauses, he told his love. She listened in silence, responding only in tighter grasps and sobs she could not repress.

Her heart, in a strange agony of grief, was communing with itself. She found in this sad event a revelation and a revolution in one. How different was this declaration from the ones he had courted and intended playing upon. And up to the new-found love in her heart came the cry, "You have murdered him."

A long silence followed, and Bob, feeling the hot tears falling on his brow, tried to smother down the groans the fierce pain wrung from him, and looked up with an expression of loving tenderness no words could express. She saw his increased paleness, heard his shortened breathings, and clasping him to her, she said :

"Oh ! Mr. Ellersly—oh ! Bob, don't die.   It is killing me."

Vain appeal ! Death's higher claim was closing in upon his heart.   He gave one more look, shut his eyes, a shudder quivered through his frame, then all was still.

The sun glimmered brightly on the wet laurel leaves, the mocking-bird sang in the cedar near, and the great world rolled on in endless life, as it ever does, regardless of the comedies and tragedies we mortals enact.

The driver and escort of the ambulance, hurrying down the road, heard as they turned the bend only the low wail of a broken-hearted woman.   For once a funeral procession had only its real mourners, for Bang, as brave a man as ever stood unmoved under fire, wept as a child.

Twenty years after, business called me to this part of the Shenandoah Valley, and I not only breakfasted at the old stone inn, but I visited the rude burying-ground to look on Bob Ellersly's last resting-place. As I entered I saw saw a carriage at the old gateway with a colored driver in livery, and inside I met a slender gray-haired woman coming from the graves. I caught only a glimpse of a pale, hollow-cheeked mourner, as she passed me.

I found the sexton busy digging a grave for a new occupant, and asking him to show me that of the Union officer he clambered out and led the way.   To my surprise I was shown a handsome monument of marble, consisting of a pedestal and broken column. I was the more amazed to find it garnished with rare flowers, and inscribed on the base I read :

SACRED TO THE MEMORY
OF ROBERT ELLERSLY, U. S. A., WHO FELL
FIGHTING FOR HIS FLAG AND COUNTRY
11TH OF AUGUST, 1862.

"Why, who erected this monument ?" I asked.

"Thar's whar you git me," responded the sexton, "for I don't know. It come up from Baltimore ready made and we was ordered to put it up.   That's all."

" Well, who strewed these flowers ? "

"Same as afore—don't know. Every Decoration Day, as they calls it, that female critter turns up, strews, an' cries, an' then vamooses. An' I must say, cries us much now as at fust."

For fear my readers will think me guilty of a wild exaggeration, let me call their attention to the fact that a woman will carry a dead lover in her heart for twenty years, when she is sure to quarrel with a live one within six months.

PETER PEPPERTON'S FOURTH O' JULY TRIUMPH.

NOVEL II.

THE Fourth o' July is a day set apart by the citizens of this blessed country on which to glorify themselves and mutilate their offspring. While the parents exalt their horn, in more senses than one, and declare, one unto the other, with much vociferation, that we are the bravest, smartest, and highest-toned people on the face of the earth, with the best government under the sun, their male offspring of tender age, armed with Chinese crackers, toy cannon and pistols, make the day hideous, and in their patriotic excitement burn out their dear eyes, blow off their sweet noses, and in many instances climb the golden stair in a very hasty and unseemly manner.

Were these accidents confined to the little actors, we might deplore their mutilations and early deaths, but we would be comforted with the thought that the tender patriots had themselves to blame, if any blame attaches to the patriotic custom. But, unfortunately, many consequences occur beyond the range of youthful exuberance. Frightened horses dash off to utter destruction with patriarchs on wheels. Women, in holiday attire, have found themselves in flames as well and no fire escape available, while cities have been burned and millions of property destroyed, all for the gratification, in a barbarous way, of young America.

Any attempt at a mitigation of the nuisance is met with opposition from the parents themselves, who claim that it is well to have patriotism developed in the children. But why should it take such a wild form as Chinese crackers and horse-pistols? Why not set the day apart as one devoted to a general breaking of window-panes? Let it be promulgated, as the law, that on the great Fourth every kid in the land, to illustrate his noisy patriotism, shall smash with pebbles all the windows in sight. This would be less dangerous and offensive than the powder business, and quite as sensible.

I never could comprehend why, in this patriotic demonstration, we should pattern after the Chinese and have it go off in loud, disagreeable noise and foul odors. Among savage nations it is common to become a nuisance while rejoicing, but civilized races take their joy and exhibit their rejoicing in a civilized way. Processions with banners and sweet music, festivals, in which wives and children take part, occupy the day, while at night artistic displays of fireworks please the multitude. The child that, on such occasions, should bang off a pistol or rack the nerves with that barbarous combination of red paper and powder, called a Chinese cracker, would be seized and thrashed on sight. The little fiend would find it unpleasant for days after to hinge on its centre, so as to come to a sitting position.

Every Fourth o' July gives me a realizing appreciation of Lamb's humor, to be found in the question he propounded for a debating society, to wit : " Was Herod as bad a character as history represents ? " I turn then to Hood's letter from the bachelor brother, who, in view of the prophesied earthquake, was written to by his sister in the country, proposing to put her children under his care at London. The poor man answered : " Dear sister, send up the earthquake, and keep the children."

There is but one celebration of the Fourth I treasure in memory, and that because of the ludicrous incidents that survive the recollection of the noise.

I was a law student under my illustrious father, who had retired from the profession he adorned to a quiet farm-life in the valley of the Mac-o-chee. My brother student was Tom Gallagher, and together we delved in those beastly commentaries known to the world as Blackstone. As all science is based on terms and a supposed reason for them, Blackstone is invaluable to the dull fellows, who accept his absurd definitions without being able to detect their absurdity, and take sound for sense.

At the time I write of law was regarded as a science and treated as such. The bar was composed of men who came to the practice from honest toil, who split rails and ploughed the ground for means on which to secure enough education to act as schoolmasters, and who then taught in the winter so as to be able to study for their profession in the summer. Hard-handed, knotty-headed fellows, they made our judges, members of Congress and leaders of the people, and were generally as earnest and solemn as mules.

We had debating societies in those days, and one night of every week in the winter the neighbors would gather in the country school house, dimly lit with tallow dips, and hear great orators discuss such grave questions as to which caused the most evil to humanity, war or intemperance ; or whether Cæsar or St. Paul was the greater man, or any kindred question capable of presenting two sides. The subject chosen a week in advance, the orators selected, and the advocates designated to think aloud on their legs came around with authorities, and fairly lifted the roof with their eloquent utterances. These were selected for either side by the president of the society, who had to decide at the end of the debate which carried off the tr umph. I observed that each orator succeeded in convincing himself, whether he captured the audience or not, and it was no uncommon circumstance for the eloquent sons of thunder to appeal, after adjournment, to their muscle, and treat the valley to sundry darkened eyes and bloody noses.

For the position of orator on the Fourth I am attempting to chronicle, we were all candidates.. The committee of citizens chosen to arrange the coming celebration of vociferous patriotism, after due deliberation, gave the place to one Andrew Jackson Fossett. Now, Andrew J. was a young man lately admitted to the bar, of a consumptive make, who ran mainly to voice. Set on end at any time, he had only to open his large mouth to pour out a stream of sound that would discount a steam-whistle and put a saw-mill to the blush. He possessed a vocabulary of long words that fairly dazed his audience.

There was something more in this contest for place than a mere exhibit of patriotic thunder. The valley possessed a lovely little country girl, who for a brief period of her existence answered to the name of Pop Sloan. Of medium height, slender as a sylph, she had the bloom of youth grafted on a delicacy of make rare to the fields of our pastoral regions. She was as pretty, to use a country expression, "as a painted wagon," or to put it stronger, as "a Missouri mule."

To make her attractions, if possible, stronger, she was the sole heiress to all old Sloan's possessions. The citizen thus designated was a man of various occupations. He kept tavern and a thorough-bred of Connestogy origin. He was postmaster and auctioneer ; but his great claim to distinction came in on the fact that he was the paternal author of the divine Pop—short for Polly, and a villainous corruption of Mary.

The venerable and many-sided Sloan appreciated his possession. He knew that Pop, gotten up regardless, and waiting on the table, active, smiling, and amiable, blinded his guests to the weak coffee, strong butter, heavy biscuits, and rancid bacon, for which they had to pay in hard cash and a harder indigestion.

He countenanced all of Pop's many admirers, careful to favor no one, as he sought the custom of all. "Ye'll have to git up mighty early in the mornin'," he was wont to say, "to catch my Pop, and I ain't a-goin' to gin any fellow a lift—for tain't fair."

Among these suitors were two who seemed to be favored more than the others by Pop herself. One was the oratorical limb of the law, the young man of the wonderful vocal organs, Andrew Jackson Fossett, Esq., and the other a country youth answering to the name of Peter Pepperton. Peter, or, as he was generally called, Pete, was a tall, stout, ruddy-cheeked fellow, well known and popular for his sense of humor and rough, but good-natured power of retort. Pete was one of our debating orators, and when he rose to speak a ripple of laughter would run over the audience in reponse to the broad grin with which he began his "discourse." And many were the laughs that followed at his quaint, humorous way of treating the arguments offered by his opponents.

I became acquainted with this love affair at an early day and in a queer manner. I met Pete in the woods one afternoon when he was felling timber. Inviting me to sit beside him on a stump he gave me his confidence.

"I want that gal, Donk." for that was the twist he gave my unfortunate name, "and I'm going to git her or break a trace—and if I don't I'm going to git up and git myself."

"What do you mean, Pete?"

"I mean to pull out o' this neck o' woods, and go to San Jo."

And the poor fellow's face took on a rueful look, so foreign to it that he seemed another man.

"Well, how are you getting on in your git, Pete?"

"There's where you git me. Derned if I know. Sometimes she's sweet on me, and then agin she ain't. Derned if I don't think she's more in the breechin' than the collar, and all on account of that ornary cuss Andy Fossett. You see he sorter outshines me. He's picking up lots of money at 'Fountin, and bucks round in store clothes all the time. I ain't got 'em only for Sunday, and then I ain't used to 'em. He is. Then he comes down on Sunday, my day, in a spanking rig, and takes her out a-riding, and the Lord alone knows what's happening in them rides," and a vexed expression came over the poor fellow's face, from which the perspiration fairly rolled.

"Why, Pete, you can have my rig any time you want it."

"Thank you, Donk; but she'd know it wasn't mine, and then I wouldn't fit the harness. I mean," he continued, seeing my puzzled look, "that the thing wouldn't hitch harmonious. You see them oxen? Well, you go to 'em and speak gently like, as you would to a hoss, and they won't move. But let me take the gad and fling it over 'em, with an oath or two, and they'll bend to it unanimous. See?"

"I think so."

"Now that ornary son o' Satan has taken to writin' her letters —longest sort, and full of honey. She reads 'em to me. I thought I'd try it on, too, and I got a book from Miller's store that was just the thing. Here it is."

He took from his coat-pocket, hanging on a sapling, a copy of the "Complete Letter-Writer," and opening on page 18 showed me a model of a letter from a young man to a young lady, making proposal of marriage. It began, "Respected Miss," and was in every respect a cast-iron model.

"Well," continued Pete, "I copied that out in my best hand-write, on pink paper, and carried it to her myself. Just as I was going to hand it over, skin my buttons if I didn't see that identical book on the table. I just husked my letter, quick as a shake of a sheep's tail. She asked me what I had there, and I said, oh. nothing but some verses for her—but I guessed Andy Fossett was a-filling the demand in that line. She gin a little scornful laugh, like, and said Andy was a beautiful writer—cuss him!'"

"She said cuss him?"

"Oh! dern it, no, I thought it. Now, Donk, I want you to help me."

"With all my heart, Pete. Shall I make love for you to the girl?"

"Thunder! no. You would put in pounds for yourself for every ounce you gave me. I'll tell you how. Folks say, Donk, you have more larning than common-sense. That's a lie, of course. How can a man have larning without sense? I want you to write me a bully love-letter, and I'll copy it. You know how to do it. You can do anything but make yourself useful, and you're right about that. Ef a monkey could be taught to hoe he wouldn't be a show in a red coat. You write me that letter, and I'll go to town next Saturday and give Bill Smith the cussedest licking he ever got for lying about you the way he does."

I declined the punishment offered my enemy in my behalf, but promised the letter. This did not save William S., however. He was somewhat surprised to find himself denounced as a reptile and liar, who was not to be permitted to promulgate slanders on his (Peter's) particular friend. And to emphasize these casual remarks William S. was given a free admission to certain fireworks more dazzling than pleasant. William, to his credit be it recorded, used due diligence, and came off second best only after a general engagement that was much admired.

The love-letter was written in choice phrase, and garnished with elegant extracts from Byron and Shelley. I was rather proud of my work, and, giving it to Pete, assured him that it was simply splendid, and if it did not fetch the divine Polly there was no use trying. When I saw Pete's copy I was disgusted to find that he had not only interpolated certain ardent expressions of his own, but had eliminated my sweet poetry, substituting some of his own selection, such as

> The rose is red, the violet's blue,
> Sugar is sweet and so are you.

When I remonstrated Pete said : "Oh, look here, Donk, them flights of yours are high pints, and mountainous, but Pop'd know I didn't come by 'em honestly, and I don't believe she'd grapple 'em anyway."

I permitted the letter to go, and a few days after the divine Pop came into our vine-clad, maple-shaded office, and requested a word with me in private. I looked at my brother student, but he declined taking the hint, so I invited the fair creature to a stroll in the garden. Seating myself on the rustic bench I said :

"Well, Miss Polly, what can I do for you ? "

She blushed crimson, and in blushing took on a grace that was perfectly bewitching. Her silken eyelashes dropped over her dreamy brown eyes, like fringed mist over moonbeams, while her pert little nose, borrowing expression from the coral cleft of a mouth, seemed to be asserting composure amid confusion. Suddenly, putting her hand in her bosom, she brought out Pete's letter and thrust it at me.

"Hello," said I, through my mental telephone, "has the little rogue discovered our fraud ? " But no. she immediately said, somewhat hurriedly, "There's a letter writ me by Pete. It's first-rate. I didn't believe Pete had it in him."

I pretended to read, and having completed the pretence, said that it was the finest thing of the sort I had ever seen. I offered it to her.

" No," she said, "you keep it."

" Why should I keep poor Pete's love-letter, Miss Polly? He'd kill me."

" Well," she said, turning her comely head away, "I want you to answer it for me. I don't want Pete to think I can't give as good as he sends. You help me ; you can do it, and not try."

" But, Miss Polly, he will know my writing."

" Not after I copy it. I write a good hand enough, but I can't compose worth a cent, and then I ain't used to such highfalutin' flub-dubs."

By Jove, I thought, here's business—answering my own letter, and a prospect ahead of carrying on a voluminous correspondence. I consented, and as a reward for my proposed services the little rogue permitted me to girdle—as the country lads called it —her slender waist and imprint a kiss on her rosy mouth.

" Say," she added, extricating herself from my rather ardent embrace, "while you're at it, you may as well answer some of these," and she put Lawyer Fossett's letters in my hand.

"Now, Miss Polly," I cried, "which of these two love-sick swains do you favor?"

"I don't care a button for them. They just make me sick with their palaver. If they only knew how to act, like some people, who don't seem to care for me, it would be better for them," and the little coquette shot a glance at me from under her eyelashes that made my heart jump to one side, like a colt shying at a red petticoat. For an innocent, inexperienced country girl to wing a fellow like that, knocked me dizzy. I made a bolt at her, but she shot under my arm and disappeared round a clump of lilacs, with a musical, ringing little laugh that told of her keen appreciation of the fun, and my dire discomfiture.

What volumes of love-letters I wrote, to and from myself—on the side of Pete, poor fellow, who never suspected, and in response to the passionate Fossett's. All the while I found myself getting more entangled in the meshes of the web this rustic beauty wound about me.

Talk about the world's masters of diplomacy, there is more subtle art and power in a girl just out than any ever possessed by the Talleyrands and Metternichs of history. To see through one, and yet remain unseen ; to be cool, collected, and shrewd in the hottest contests, to win through inimitable tact the subject dealt with, and make the wise-t man play the fool, give me a woman as she comes from the hands of nature.

With all the advantage I possessed of Polly's confidence, I failed to make any progress, and was kept at a certain distance that always seemed to be about closing and never closed.

My friend Pete seemed satisfied with my love-letters written him through Polly, and often brought them to me for a better interpretation of their meaning, as well as answer. I did not want the pretty Polly to marry either. I was in love with her, in a certain fashion, and feared Fossett more than Pete; so trying a little diplomacy in my part, I threw cold water on Andrew J. while I encouraged Pete.

The time came for the celebration of the Fourth, and great was the preparation thereof. All the farmers far and near agreed to fetch provisions, which meant an unlimited supply of "chicken fixins," pies and cakes, heavy enough to give dirt-eating Indian diggers a dreadful indigestion. An old smooth-bore, said to have seen service in the war of '12, was borrowed and a gun-squad organized, with the aged Choptank for captain, and it was much surmised that if the ancient Choptank, who "fit under Perry," could remain sober until after the salute of thirteen guns the salute would be a success. Otherwise it was surmised there would be casualties, and some people's arms and legs would be sacrificed to the old smooth-bore and the Fourth. A brass band of six discordant pieces from 'Fountain had volunteered, and gave assurances they would play the "Star Spangled Banner," "Hail Columbia," and "Yankee Doodle," so as to distinguish one from the other. A moral showman was licensed to exhibit his "natural curiosities," which consisted of a fat woman and anacondas, the skeleton man, and a bottled pig possessed of two heads and an assortment of tails.

Such a Fourth had never before been celebrated in the valley, and probably never will be again.

Unfortunately, within a week of the great occasion, the eloquent orator of the day, Andrew Jackson Fossett, was taken down with a violent attack of the quinsy. He could not speak above a whisper, and could not swallow at all. Of course, he had to be eliminated from the proceedings. It was too late to engage another. No one of us, on such short notice, would undertake the duty. Now a Fourth without an orator was "Hamlet" without Hamlet, King, Queen. Ophelia, or even Yorick's skull.

To the amazement of every one, suddenly Peter Pepperton volunteered. It was Hobson's choice, and Pete was accepted.

"Do you want me to help you?" I asked the volunteer the day he was accepted.

"No, Donk. Got a better lay-out than that. Keep you're off eye on me. I'm goin' to git her this time or break a trace. Stay in the high grass till ye hear me yell, then tumble out an' see big Ingin."

The Fourth came, big with the fate of Peter and his love. Assembled in Whopple's grove, the farmers' and farmers' wives and children, gotten up in their store-clothes, perspired in profusion while listening to the six pieces of a brass-band, that made up in blowing all they lacked in music. Captain Choptank, with his gun-squad and old smooth-bore, at intervals startled the jays and our assembly with a mouthing roar that to'd in thunder of the glorious struggle of our fathers for independence. The venerable Choptank was very drunk. even at that early hour, but he seemed quite as efficient drunk as sober.

The Rev. Doolittle Stubbs opened the ceremonies with an eloquent address to the "Throne of Grace." Then followed the reading of that elegant compos tion from the pen of the immortal Jefferson. called the Declaration of Independence, and then Peter came to the front. in gorgeous apparel and a high state of perspiration. Assuming a bold, pugilistic position, peculiar to Fourth of July orators, he paused before giving the British lion one in the countenance to take us into his confidence, by saying : " Feller-citizens, ladies, and gentlemen." His opening sentence was lost in old Choptank's roar from the smooth-bore.

When the noise had subsided, I discovered that Pete had launched the ship of state. The S. of S. is alwlays launched in a Fourth of July oration. It has rough weather, of course. The clouds darken. the thunder rolls, the mountain waves mount to the skies. But there is a hand at the helm, and he steers the bark, laden with the hopes of humanity, safely to its harbor. This introduces Washington, and Washington is a Moses, a star, a mountain peak, and a god.

Washington, of course, lets fly the American eagle. Pete flew the eagle for all it was worth. He had one wing on the Alleghenies, the other on the Rockies, while the tail o'ershadowed the Canadas—and while screaming and soaring in the most terrible manner the British lion was seen in full retreat across the stormy seas, quite sick, and fearfully demoralized.

Pete was acquitting himself with rare excellence. He had suddenly broken out like an Indian war in full bloom as a great orator. I never had heard such a volume of sounds, never such a collection of many-syllabled words. The audience applauded every sentence, and Choptank's cannon roared in response.

In the midst of this the sick Andrew J. Fossett appeared, and was helped kindly to a seat. His neck was done up in a huge poultice, and his face was pale as death. Suddenly the sick man staggered to his feet. His face reddened to the tint of a boiled lobster and his eyes glared with the gleam of a maniac. He could only utter shrieks, while he gesticulated like a windmill struck by a cyclone.

He was delirious, all thought, and kind but strong arms carried him away, while Pete in his peroration had Columbia soaring and tyranny sinking in the dark vortex of coming time. "Upward and onward!" cried Pete, "the star of liberty gleamin' with dazzlin' refulgence, in her crown of glory, casting its lightning ray adown the coming centuries of untold time, reflaring, reflecting, *ad infinitum*, onward and upward forever. *E pluribus unum!*"

Pete closed. The audience shouted. The women waved handkerchiefs, the men cotton umbrellas. Choptank fired his last charge, and the band struck up—blame me if I know what it struck up, but it was a noise, to which the assembly scattered, and I saw Pete, with Polly upon his arm, march off to the collation, with her sweet face beaming in love and triumph.

Two weeks thereafter they were married.

Andrew Jackson Fossett was very ill for a month thereafter. When convalescent he sank into a pro'ound gloom, as if his life were blighted. He proved this by throwing up his profession and becoming that elegant enemy of man known as a hotel clerk, with a diamond breast-pin, at a fashionable hotel in a distant city.

Years after Pete confided to me a startling fact that solved the mystery of this strange affair. *He had stolen his rival's oration.*

LUNY LEN.

NOVEL III.

The railroad station known as Glen Cove is one of the dreariest this side of that final abode said to be extremely sultry, where all presidents, directors, and other railway officials, more especially ticket-agents, fetch up and finish their labors. Were it not so hard on Mugby Junction, I should say Glen Cove was the Mugby Junction of America. Indigestion is kept there, like fixed ammunition in the quartermaster's department, to serve out at a moment's notice to hungry and insane passengers, and it is safe, for the trains carry the sufferers to die in distant localities.

One hot, sunny day of midsummer I found myself anticipating the punishment due for sins and shortcomings in this world by waiting for an eastern-bound train long overdue, as if the trains, like the passengers, disliked approaching the depot at which I suffered.

A surly telegrapher, also ticket agent, who jerked lightning, shot insults and tickets through a hole at people, told me, after an hour's cross-examination that was very cross, that my train had brought up in a corn-field, and I could not possibly get away by rail before midnight.

Now, what to do with myself from the noon of this information to the noon of night was a question that sorely perplexed me. I had no book, no papers, no anything to relieve the dull monotony of that awful wait.

I wandered listlessly about the dirty depot and platform. Both were hot enough to roast potatoes in the shade. I gazed on—nay, I studied all the colored bills, giving picturesque views of various towns, and telling in assorted type the advantages each had over the other—the only bit of amusement I had, and it was very mild. I found in guessing at the missing letters of a bill which read "Rough Line to Chicago," some scamp had cut out the initial

"Th" when the bill had originally read, "Through Line to Chicago."

While upon the platform gazing at an accommodation train just in, that was awaiting its conductor who was leisurely ge'ting orders from the telegrapher, I was attracted by a noisy crowd of men and boys. gathered about a young fellow whose face indicated the idiotic condition that originated their entertainment.

He was a tall, broad shouldered, well-formed youth, and well dressed for one in his condition. But he had his clothes half-buttoned, in the loose, reckless manner of his class, while his face, without its intellectual outlook, was regular in feature, and one could see, had there been a brain back of it, would have been eminently handsome. As anxiety and care had ceased writing its record of age upon his face, it was difficult to tell his age. He had the form of a man and the face of a child.

" It's the opinion of this crowd, Len," said the blacksmith to the idiot, "that you can beat that locomotive in a race from here to the tunnel, and we have bet ten thousand dollars on it."

The poor fellow's dead face lit up with an expression of delight, so pitiable that it would have disarmed any other crowd than the one engaged in chaffing him. He gazed wistfully at the huge locomotive that stood hissing in the hot sun as if wrathful at the delay, and then he turned to the cruel crowd as if the suggestion was slowly working its way through his poor crippled brain.

" Go in, Len," cried one of the crowd, " we've got our money on you, and you're bound to win."

" We'll give you fifty yards the start. You keep on the track," cried the blacksmith, "and the thing can't pass you."

I could scarcely believe these scoundrels were in earnest, when the surly engineer gave the last bang to his noisy bell, exploded a short snort from the locomotive in the way of warning, and to my astonishment I saw the idiot, throwing off his coat, start down the track ahead of the train. Fortunately the engineer caught sight of the poor fellow, and checking the speed of the locomotive, began ringing him off the track. This was responded to by the idiot bawling out with great glee : "Come on with your old tea-kettle!" and the brutal crowd cheered and roared with laughter.

The crowd, keeping along with the train, cheered lustily, and the lunatic "spurted," as they say in a boat-race—that is, shot ahead and exhibited considerable power as a racer by the speed with which he got over the ground. The engineer, infuriated at the delay, put on speed and rattled after. But he was upon a down-grade, and, fearful of overtaking the unfortunate, he almost immediately put on the brakes and checked up again.

By this time heads were thrust out of windows and the platforms crowded by passengers whose excitement became noisy and intense as they discovered that it was a human being instead of a cow that impeded their progress. As for the idiot, he paused only long enough to indulge in a jeering laugh and a gesture that was more irritating than decent.

The crowd of brutal loafers that exhibited more industry in accompanying the race on this occasion than they had probably manifested in making an honest living for a year previous, went tearing along each side of the locomotive, laughing, shouting, cheering on the idiot, while hurling all sorts of exasperating epithets at the engineer, who, by this time, was nearly blind with rage.

At this moment the conductor made his appearance, and, crawling out upon the tender, began throwing lumps of coal at the boy, as the engineer, putting on steam, drew near the poor fellow.

Fortunately the conductor's aims were not well taken, for had the young man been knocked down the locomotive would have undoubtedly run over him.

From this the rough autocrat of the train soon desisted, for the idiot's backers, with an American sense of fair play that animates even the roughest of our brutes, began pelting the conductor with stones, each pebble sent with the accuracy of a rifle-shot at that part of his animal economy where the legs end and the body begins. He retreated hurriedly to the engine-house, where he rubbed his person in a comical way with one hand, while with the other he assuaged his wrath by a furious ringing of the bell. The engineer seconded his efforts by letting off short shrieks and keeping the locomotive frightfully close upon the heels of the wretched youth.

Having begun life with a strange disposition to take upon myself the ills of others, and finding such practice extremely unpleasant and useless, I have gradually trained myself into the other
extreme, and generally bear the misfortunes of my friends with a
philosophical indifference that is very composing. On this occasion, however, I forgot my cynicism and found myself running
under that broiling sun, shaking my fist, with my heart in my
mouth, at the conductor, and demanding in the most authorita-
tive manner that he stop the train.

From the depot to the tunnel was about half a mile ; to accomplish this distance the train and idiot occupied some four minutes.
The passengers, crowded at windows and on the platforms, took as
lively an interest in the affair as the entire population of Glen
Cove that accompanied the train and backed the idiot. It was a
Godsend to the passengers, and they expressed their satisfaction by
the liveliest betting and cheers, first for the locomotive and then
for its strange competitor.

It was neck-and-neck between life and the locomotive. A
false step, a stumble, and the huge mass of roaring, throbbing iron
would have gone crushing over the frail body of the man who so
strangely impeded its progress. And such result was imminent ;
for the poor fellow, exhausted by excitement and over-exertion,
staggered at times, and at times reeled as if about to fall, in a way
to make me shudder.

That such would probably have been the result became
painfully apparent, when an abrupt and somewhat unexpected
termination was put to the cruel sport. The man stationed at
the mouth of the tunnel and employed to keep its murky depths
clear of obstructions, suddenly seized the youth, at the risk of his
own life, and threw him with some violence to one side. Such
was the effort that both rolled over, and the huge locomotive,
giving a shrill scream of triumph, dived into the tunnel, f llowed
by the long train, that disappeared as if the earth had opened and
swallowed it.

I sat down at the mouth of the subterranean excavation quite
exhausted as the crowd dispersed. and from the mouth of the
dark entrance was pleased to find a cool, damp air that came out in

puffs, as if a dragon were coiled up within and panted out its cold, clammy breath. I asked the old watchman a series of idle questions, of a statistical sort, such as a man under the circum· stances always indulges in. He grunted out the exact length of the tunnel, the time required to construct it, the accidents that occurred within his remembrance, and altogether, in response to my leading questions, exhibited a good deal of information on tunnels. For a man to know one thing well is a power. It is bet-ter, however, to believe you know some one thing and impart the information to your friends. It is a bore at best and just as well when it takes the shape of a tunnel.

Having exhausted the hole in the ground—and really, come to think of it, there was nothing in it—I spoke of the late race.

"Crazy jackass!" quoth the sententious guardian of the excavation; "he'll git killed yet, and sooner the better for all consarned."

"Why, do they often put him up to that?"

"No, not frequent. They do it on t at train sometimes, for they hate the conductor. Onct, long ago, it wasn't needed. He used to run ahead of every t ain, clear through the tunnel, a warnin' people off. They switched that out uv him. Now the ornary cusses puts him up to it."

"Queer sort of insanity."

"Isn't it? and he was onct a bright feller—a rale schollard."

"Indeed?"

"Yes, was onct, but left his senses in this tunnel."

"Why, how was that?"

"Well, you see, he's the son of old Judge Conrad, of these parts—only child at that—and was sent to college, and no end of trouble taken and money spent to fini-h and furnish up his intellects. When he came home to study law, what does he do but take after a little girl named Mary Grubbs, da'ter of the cooper, an' she was poor as a pig an' purty as a painted wagon. Well, I guess she was about the handsomest critter in this part of the vineyard. Len Conrad was struck, I tell you, after Polly, as we called her, an' I don't wonder; for her hair was as soft and light as silk on early corn, an' she had the handsomest teeth, an'

the biggest, wonderfullest dark eyes, an' an angeliferous skin.
But neither she nor her old cooperin' dad had a cent, so the
Conrads, bein' toploftical mahogany high posters, just shut down
on her."

" The old, old story."

" I don't know ef it's so old. Per'aps you've heerd it afore, an'
I can save my wind."

" I mean that the course of true love never does run smooth."

" Oh ! that's it, is it ? "

" No offence, old man. But proceed with your yarn and tell
me how Len Conrad left his senses in the tunnel."

" That's what I was a comin' to when you put in your chin
music. When Len found the family was forninst the courtin' he
took to meetin' her unbeknownst. That was found out, and then
it was decreed that Len should be sent to Yourope. The evenin'
upon Len's departure he meets his girl, av course, an' they mean-
dered naterly a li tle too late, an' undertook to make a short-cut to
the cooper house through the tunnel. I saw the doves go in. She
was a-leanin' on his shoulder a-weepin, an' he looked as if he'd lost
his mother-in-law."

" Mother-in law ! "

" That's a little joke o' mine, mister. I mean he looked like a
canned funeral. I warned 'em not to try the tunnel, for it was
close on to the time for the lightnin' express. But they didn't
heed or hear me—jes' kept on in. After they had left I got that
oneasy I took my lantern an' run arter 'em. Jes' as I came
in sight the infernal thing came a roarin' past Glen Cove—it don't
stop there—an' I heard the whistle as the death on wheels plunged
into the tunnel. I jammed the wall, I tell yez. I could see Len push
his girl agin the same so the train might pass and not touch, an'
like a flash I saw her tear away. Now, whether she was scart and
didn't know what she was about, or wanted to kill herself, can't be
known, but she shot right in front ov that train. I saw the head-
light shine like a flash uv lightn'ng on a white, frightened face as
I crowded back ag'n the wall, an' then with a roar like thunder, an'
the whole thing seemed wiped out as if a sponge had sorter
sponged us out. I heard the train's thunder sort of spread as it

left the tunnel, as if soundin' the murder over the land, an' I stood there in a sort uv a daze listnin' to that roar die out in the distance. When I come round, which I did in a minit, I ran on. I stumbled over po r Len, lyin' as if dead, an' then I run up and down at least twict before I saw a heap that looked like a bundle of rags soaked in bl od, an' will you believe, the bundle moved. It was only a quiver, an' all was still. She d dn't make a lovely corpse when we got it togther. Some people sickened an' fainted when they saw it."

"And Len?"

"We carted him home. The doct rs could not find any bones broken, cuts, or hurt inside or out, but he lay sorter stoopid six weeks and then got up an' has been looney ever since."

"Poor fellow."

"Should think so. Queerest thing about the poor chap was that he took to runnin' ahead uv trains, goin' through the tunnel a-warnin' people off. He sorter got that hammered out uv him."

"The old folks learned a lesson, eh?"

"Not much; can't teach sich old stoopids much. They do say the old Jedge has softenin' uv the brain, but I don't believe he had any to soften."

HANDLED GOODS.

MAKING a hasty escape from the Green Briar White Sulphur Springs, where the wretched fare poisoned the day and the noise at night robbed one of sleep, I took refuge at the Old Sweet Chalybeate Springs. Next to the Congressional Library at Washington, this place is the least frequented and quietest resort known to Southern humanity. A few fashionable people willing ever to pay for their exclusiveness ; a few noted men whose pockets accord with their taste and really seek for rest ; a number of old habitués given to quiet games of poker and silent drinking ; quite a number of invalids making a hard fight for life, compose the patrons of the Old Sweet, and the quiet repose was so startling that I felt like one escaping from a Donnybrook fair who finds himself in an old moss-grown cemetery.

Sitting one morning on one of those instruments of torture called a rustic bench at the Spring, I saw a fair lady coming towards us along the elm-shaded walk, escorted by a youth got up in white flannel, punctuated by a blue necktie, and as he carried his light panama hat in hand, his blond hair appeared evenly parted on that bulbous termination to a spinal column called a head. The young man had an eye-glass screwed in before one optic, that being held to its place by muscular effort, gave to one side of his face the appearance of a much wrinkled monkey's, while the other was as smooth and youthful as an infant's.

I knew the lady—Miss Adelaide De Pros. She was for many seasons a belle at Washington, and lifting my hat at her approach, got in return a smile of recognition that flashed over her fair, pale face like sunlight over ice. As she sipped at a glass of water her escort gave her, my mind went back over the years to the time when this lovely girl appeared to rise on society like a new-born Venus from a foamy sea of skirts. I use this well-worn figure because of the fascinating freshness the little maiden gave the fashionable world. Of course her family and the remnant of wealth left from the civil war gave her position, but the winning qualities were all her own. Her great beauty was enhanced by a strange combination of frankness and diffidence that made her at once shy and confiding.

Ah me, social life has changed for the worse since that day, and especially at Washington. Time was when beauty reigned at our capital as wealth reigns to-day. I remember when Miss Woodbury had a greater following than Henry Clay. The advent of a fresh belle was heralded, and when she came a way opened of itself before her in ball-rooms and at receptions, where a general silence was followed by murmurs of admiration. That was the day of bouquets and serenades, duels and public adorations. In the smoking-rooms, cloak-rooms, and barber shops of House and Senate, eminent solons interspersed political jokes with stories of fair women, and eloquent members looked up to the galleries, not in fear of journalists, but to get inspiration from lovely faces and bright eyes. The fair forms and the eloquent solons have long since mouldered into dust, and in their places the money-getters of our busy life are the actors who move an empire and tread to earth, as under the hoofs of animals, the poetry of life.

But to return to our mutton. Miss Adelaide's season ended in a little romance wherein she fell captive to the wooing of a Southern youth, about the worst selection she could have made from the army of men who eagerly sought her hand. She became engaged, and her father consented only on an agreement from the young people that the marriage should be deferred for a year. Before the year was out the lover broke his troth, and married a wealthy widow, so much older than himself that she could have been his mother, and might well be counted on to be his sainted Maria before many years of ill-usage.

Miss Adelaide did not sicken and die of unfortunate true love. She had too tough a fibre for that, and too much self-respect to marry from pique the first eligible offer. The lesson taught her made a heartless coquette. She found amusement in playing with hearts, while she kept her own untouched.

It was interesting to study the lovely face as through season after season the girlish freshness faded. It gave place to an intellectual outlook almost as fascinating. Men fell as readily in love with her as before, but while she favored many she committed herself to no one, and stories were told of promising men ruined by her as she dismissed them right and left. It was said that some took to business and others to drink. Of course all these stories of her fatal influence were got up by envious rivals. Men have gone to drink and cards and ruined themselves, but never from love. That would have been their end, of course, had never an Adelaide De Pros crossed their paths.

Time was kind to Adelaide, and the winning beauties of her face disappeared only to give place to others, but these others were not of the sort to win eligible husbands, and at thirty the beautiful woman found herself yet a belle, "followed, flattered, sought, and sued," but not by men from whom she could select a husband. Of late she had devoted herself to religion and literature, but neither in piety nor books could she see for herself a future that would render her either successful or content. She had not entirely exhausted either Europe or our own continent, but she had exhausted herself, and depressed in spirit and health, she had come to the Old Sweet under the care of General Janson and family, with nothing but a blooded horse and riding-habit to detract her attention from cards, meditation, and a care of her health.

As she walked away, a voice at my elbow said, "Handled goods." I turned with an angry interrogation point in my eyes to stare at Hamilton Porkus, of Chicago.

This young man had made himself familiar to every guest at the Spring. He did not rest with these, but was on the best of terms with the diamond-breasted man of the clerk's office, whose insolence of manner made every one long for a shotgun ; with that gorgeous creature the head waiter of the dining-room, who made one feel as if he ought to go out and buy some new clothes ; and he had the run of the stables, where he passed the greater part of his time. Young, rather handsome, easy, good-natured and impudent, he offended nobody while failing to please any one.

The only son and heir of the late Doctor Porkus, the young

man lived to spend the million his medicated parent had accumulated through a patent pain extractor. Cool, cunning, and selfish,
the heir held well to the fortune. His earlier sorrow and disgust
came of the fact that society did not recognize his claims, and
later certain ills that flesh is heir to made him unhappy. He had
inherited enough of his father's money-getting instincts to shut
him out of an enjoyment of life. Hence travel bored him, art
and literature were dead letters to him, and, dimly conscious of
the fact that good society ignored him, he had but one ambition,
and that was to be one of that mythical world.

"Gambling," he was wont to say, "is no good. I don't want
a fellow's money, and, by God, I don't want him to have mine.
Dissipation—well, I tried that—can't stand it. At the end of last
winter I was sick to crying, as the country girls say. A friend
told me to see Fordyce Barker. I did ; he punched and pounded
me, tumbled me up and down, located my trouble in the liver,
gave me a prescription and a bill of two hundred dollars. Then
another friend said I must see Hammond. Hammond Porkus did
all Barker's punching and pounding, then he stuck pins in my legs,
looked into my eyes and said he saw an obscure disease in the
base of my brain. He saw five hundred dollars of my money at
the same time. Then I went to Leart, and he said I had the
new nervous disorder that began with a bang in the head and
ended with softening of the brain. This information cost me two
hundred dollars. Then I tried Bartholow ; he gave me twenty
minutes and a demand for two hundred and fifty. While I was
counting out the money, he told me I didn't need a physician but
a hoe-handle and skim milk. ' Go to the country,' he said, ' live
on thirty-seven and a half cents a day and earn it.' I came back
to Washington, and Garnett said I had Washington malaria that
was bottled and labelled champagne and whiskey, and advised me
to go to Old Sweet and soak it out."

This was the man that had said "handled goods" as the
beautiful Miss Adelaide swept away. As I did not like the coarse
expression, not taking it clearly, he continued :

"Handled goods, Colonel. are apt to be damaged—second-hand
any how—and a fellow wants the article fresh if he wants it at all."

"You find a good deal of handled goods at these summer re-
sorts, Mr. Porkus."

"You bet. The guls are thrown on the market, and a good
deal pawed over before taken. Don't like it. Handled goods are
apt to be damaged goods."

"You should go into the rural districts, and get some charming, fresh country lass to make you happy."

Mr. Hamilton Porkus gave a quite little laugh, and responded,
"Tried it, by Jove! No-go, Colonel; was down for an autumn
at a country house. Had a sweet little blonde pitched at me. No
chignon, by Jove! real hair on plump white shoulders; little or
no pannier; all natural as morning glories, moss-roses, and fresh
eggs. Thought my time had come. We rode and walked and
spoonied for three months. By Jove! done up that parcel in
three weeks; time flew so. Well, I popped, and she just come
down into pocket as natural and sweet and soft; well, for a week I
was in a rural heaven with an angel done up in muslin and loving
simplicity. One day I came in from a bit of gunning, and passing
by the identical summer-house where I had popped, I heard a
little cry garnished with sobs. The leaves were dropping from
that summer-house, and the wind blew so that it might be a sound
from both; but I turned in, and, by Jove! there was my rural
felicity in the arms of a tall fellow, ugly—to me—as Satan, and
wearing a bob-tailed navy-blue. When they saw me the fellow
looked fierce, and my love flabbergasted. Well, in an instant she
flopped—not in my arms, but down upon her knees, and with sob-
bing voice and streaming eyes begged me not to break her heart,
that she loved Henry Augustus. I said 'handled goods,' and as
rural felicity didn't comprehend, I said, 'Rise up, Isabella; take
her, navy-blue. Bless you, my children!'"

I give Mr. Hamilton Porkus at length, for he is the hero of
our one bit of romance. He met his fate, and a better one than
he deserved, leaving out the million accumulated from the patent
pain extractor. It came about in this wise: Mr. Hamilton Porkus
had nothing to engage his active intellect but treatment, and it was
the most natural thing in the world that he should become devoted
to the fair lady. She received his attentions graciously. They

walked in pairs, rode together, and the gossips of the resort felt a real pity for the poor youth who was being, as they said, led on to be jilted in the end.

The affair had been going on some six weeks before I arrived, and I was not slow in coming to the conclusion that Miss Addie meant business. I thought it pitiful as others did, but from a different standpoint. I saw the once famous belle, who had been fished for by some of the more famous men of the day, turned angler, and dropping an almost naked hook before the nose of this stupid inheritor of a million. She who had gone idly and wantonly through rich fields of flowers, now on a barren sand stooped to this weed. I was infinitely amused to see the delicate, fascinating way in which she approached and tempted, without appearing to do so, her proposed prize, and I wondered how far Hamilton's selfishness and cunning would protect him. I could observe that he did most of the talking, and I could well believe that she was bending her imperious impatience to a wearied hearing, under an air of intense interest, of his dull stories about himself.

In the midst of this General H., now a brilliant, successful lawyer, and lately a distinguished officer in the Confederate service, appeared among us, and became the devoted of Miss Addie. They were old friends, and poor Hamilton was completely cut out. The walks and rides and dances once his were now the property of that cool, quiet, impudent fellow. It was the old story of a loan of a lover, and to make that story short I have only to add that Hamilton wakened to find himself desperately, blindly in love. He could not sleep nor eat, and the dreaded symptoms again appeared. What with a pain in his heart and a pain in his back the poor fellow was in a bad way.

I have that in my countenance that induces people to put unprotected females under my care while travelling and drives spoonies to making me their confidant. Hamilton came to me with his grief.

"I'm stuck," he said, "I am stuck for that gul, and there's no mistake about it, and she throws me over—throws me over for that reb."

"Did you ever give her to understand your feelings?"

"Well, no ; you see when I had her all to myself I was ass enough to think she was after me. Now don't laugh. You see I've had lots of guls throwing out signals, and she's a little old and had a lively time."

"Handled goods?"

"Now don't. You see there's no nonsense about that gul ; she's all mind and gamy. But I thought she was in chase, and I just fooled along for the fun of it. But Lord, Lord, what an ass a fellow can make of himself when he thinks he isn't an ass ! That fellow comes, and she tosses me over like an old glove. I tell you I'm in a bad way, and that blarsted pain, you see, is after me."

"See here, Porkus, don't be more of an ass than you can help. That girl thinks more of you this minute than she does of that ex-reb."

"Oh ! come now ; don't chaff a sick fellow," he cried, but his face brightened and I continued :

"Yes, she is a sensible woman, and has known a good deal of the human race, and she sees that you are a good, honest-hearted fellow, one to make a wife happy, while she regards this legal skyrocket as a nice fellow to flirt with, but one to break a woman's heart in ninety days."

"Did she tell you that ?"

"Certainly not, but I can see. Now I tell you, go in and make love to her."

"I'd as soon make love to Lady Macbeth—"

"Nonsense ! she is a woman, therefore may be wooed. She is a woman, therefore may be won. I tell you what, now you go to her yonder, she is reading alone ; say that it has been some time since you have had the pleasure of a ride ; ask her to permit you to escort her to Fern Falls. As you ride along, tell her how happy she has made your visit to the Springs, that you never can forget this summer, it has been so delightful. If she takes this kindly, say that you don't know how you can be contented to leave here and her both, and—"

"Stop ! stop ! don't put in too much or I'll forget every word. I've got the beginning, and it's first-rate. If she lets me say that much, hang me if I don't bolt it all out."

"Hold hard, don't do that on horseback, it's the most awkward place to pop in the world. If you're rejected you can't get away; if you're accepted you can't embrace; horses don't understand that, and by the time you get your arm around her the animals pull you apart; and if you attempt to kiss you are joggled up and down all over the countenance, kissing the nose and chin more than any other place."

"By Jove! what a knowing cuss you are; I never thought of that."

"Make love as you ride along. At the falls you'll have to assist her to dismount; give her a little squeeze as you climb down the precipice; give one squeeze of the hand to every jump; when down just out with it; say in a sentence, ' Miss Addie, I love you— I can't live without you—will you be mine?' She will say 'no,' they always do. But don't mind that, seize her hand—kiss it— put your manly arm about her slender waist and hold on till she says 'yes.'"

"Well, I'll try it on, if I die for it."

I saw him approach the fair Addie; I saw the sweet smile start from her beautiful mouth and run over her face like the first flush of dawn, and that afternoon I saw them ride away together. The Confederate luminary undertook to put her on her horse, but she gracefully waved him away and gave her slender foot to my friend. As they rode off together I heard the Confed. deliver a long, low whistle, that expressed surprise—I may say amazement. It was the most expressive whistle ever whistled by an ex-Confederate officer and an immediate legal luminary.

That night Hamilton conducted me to the most sequestered bench on the lawn. It was ve y late. He and Miss Addie had been pacing the main walk for hours.

"Well," I said, "how did it work?"

"First-rate; but, Lord, how I did tumble through! I was stringhalted, lame, and poll-eviled all the way. I let out as we rode along how happy she had made me; it was informal, husky; I seemed to have a frog in my throat, and my heart thumped like a sledge-hammer. I had to say it twice, and then she turned and looked at me in such a curious way I blushed all over. Then she gave me a lecture two miles in length on the idle, worthless life I was leading—what I might do with my great wealth. I wanted to tell her it was all because of her. But I did get in a good thing, all my own. I told her a fellow must have somebody to help him do the right thing, a lovely, superior woman, and I never had anybody, and she said she felt sorry for me. I tell you, old fellow, she's a noble creature, and made me feel small."

"Well?"

"I helped her down and thought I'd squeeze her hand, but I hadn't the pluck. I did going down the rocks, but Cæsar Augustus! what was the use? Her little hand lay in mine cold and soft as a snow-flake, and she looked as unconscious as a gate-post. We dawdled about there, climbing rocks and gathering stuff, weedy stuff, dirty and damp, that I had to put in my pockets for her. At last, in a very wild place, I just turned on her and said, husky and jerky again, 'Miss Addie, would you mind taking a rough fellow in hand and show him how to do the right thing?' She was giving me a long, snaky weed that she said was a beautiful specimen, and I dropped it and seized her hand. Good Lord! but I was scared. She jerked away and colored up and said, 'Mr. Porkus!' as if she was going to ask me what I had to say why sentence of death should not be passed there and then, but she didn't, and I stood there like a sick calf in a thunderstorm. Then she turned and sat down on a rock, and for a devil of a time looked at the tumbling waters, pulling a weed to pieces. Then she looked up at me with a sad sort of smile and said:

"'Mr. Porkus, am I to understand that you are serious in all this, and really love me?'

"I was down by her side in a second and I seized her hand, and, Lord, how I did go on. She kept looking at the water, and I girdled her without knowing it. I don't know what happened, only she brought me up at last by saying, 'There, there, I hear people coming down the rocks; behave yourself and I will do the best I can to make you a good man and happy one.' But she was cool, I tell you."

"Handled goods, Porkus."

"Now look here, old fellow, you don't want to quarrel with me, and that's chaff on the raw."

"No, my dear fellow, on the contrary, I congratulate you; you have won the most beautiful and the noblest woman in Virginia. Your rival, the reb and immediate luminary, went off to the White Sulphur after you left, a good deal in love and deeper in liquor.

AUNT HETTY.

NATIONAL traits in their popular acceptation are national superstitions. Humanity is about the same the world over, and while the earth has its uniformity with slight differences in mountain and plain, so its products are very nearly alike. The rattlesnake of the temperate zone is the cobra of the torrid, and that strange combination set on end and called man may be black in Africa, yellow in Asia, copper-tinted in America, and white in Europe, but he is man all the same, having reason and like appetites. The boa of India is larger than the black-snake of America, but the traits are about the same, and so with men of different climes.

For ages we have had the Englishman depicted in the popular mind as a beef-eater, hearty, bluff, and brave. The Frenchman appears as a thin, excitable, dark-haired consumer of frogs. The witty, roystering, combative Irishman of the stage is the Irishman of life, while we Americans are Yankees with a nasal twang, and ready at any moment to turn our grandmother's bones into buttons. Yet the practical observer looks in vain through England for the blond beef-eater ; through France for the man who cooks frogs and lives in an excited state of *sacre bleu*. The Irish may be a rather combative people under an oppression that would stir Holland to a revolt, but the stage Irishman has an exceptional existence in real life, while the New Englanders can show, in public charities, as much generous impulse as any people on earth.

This is written because of all humanity the negro has been most clearly defined as possessed of certain traits that distinguish the race as a separate and distinct creation from the rest of humanity. This comes mainly from writers of fiction. As Cooper created the noble red-man, Bret Harte the heathen Chinee, so Mrs. Stowe and others have given us the negro. To the critic who coolly analyzes plots and characters, this building up of the negro, especially as a slave, is extremely ludicrous. It presents the strongest possible argument in favor of slavery. For dramatic effect the masters are presented to us as monsters of cruel iniquity, and the poor slaves as wonderful specimens of patient, Christian goodness. If this is the result of human servitude, such a state has done more for the sway of Christ than all the gospel teachings to a fallen race that ever were put to record. For one Uncle Tom we can well condone a hundred Legrees.

This is written not as an essay, but to introduce a strange character, deeply impressed on the mind of the writer; a negro woman, but so different from the accepted negro that to win belief I have had to call attention to some errors of superstition that forbid credence. When quite young I came to know Aunt Hetty, and had for her a feeling of mingled fear and affection difficult to understand and put in harmony. She was old, very old, when I knew her, I being then a boy, but to the last she was erect, vigorous, and positive. When so old that her hair was white, and her dimmed eyes called for spectacles, she taught herself to read, that she might have her Bible to herself, and all that Bible taught she construed into lessons that might have shamed many a learned theologian. She found no difficulty in harmonizing the God of vengeance with the Christ of love, and while tender and loving to the little ones left to her care, she was as stern as fate in the punishment of youthful wrong-doing. The keen insight of youthful character she possessed gave her a knowledge of our wicked ways, that seemed to us miraculous. There was no orchard robbed, no hen-house despoiled, no swimming on Sundays that old Aunt Hetty did not know of, and she could single out the leader with an unerring certainty that made our vigorous lying of no avail.

There was a tradition, to the effect that Aunt Hetty was an African princess, afloat, and, in our youthful eyes, she certainly had the ways of one. Tall, slender, with a skin as black as ever Africa produced, she had a quiet dignity of movement that impressed itself upon all. She had not only taught herself to read, but she had trained her tongue to a better use of the English language than shown by many of her superiors, white and educated though they were.

In all self-training Aunt Hetty had one model she studied and imitated, and that was her old master, Colonel Jacob Parnne. The individuality of this old soldier of the Revolution was so marked and strong that no one could come within its range without feeling its influence. Of Huguenot blood he was by birth and through generations a French Puritan. His keen, dark eyes, prominent Roman nose, and no less prominent chin, with his spare, upright figure, indicated that he was a man who walked with God, and walked in a very upright and soldierly manner. There were with him no questions of morality and religion. They had all been ended, judgment rendered, and the book closed when John Calvin announced the decisions of the Lord.

Entering the service as a private when the colonies rebelled against the mother country, he fought his way up, through all the great battles, to the rank of Colonel.

Colonel Jacob Parnne's reasons for this patriotic service were strictly private and his own. The political aspect of the quarrel did not interest him. The taxation without representation and all the list of other grievances he treated with contempt but as his grandfather had fled from France rather than submit to the rule of the Catholic Church, he regarded the Church of England as the bastard offspring of what he called the "scarlet woman of Rome," and against the Established Church he carried on the war. As he found no one to sympathize with him in this view of the contest, he felt that he alone was the instrument of God to carry on the war.

Next to Calvin the old Colonel believed in George Washington. The intense seriousness of the rebel General, with the imposing length of his figure, impressed his admirer to such an extent, that even the great Virginian's profanity could not shake his confidence. On the contrary, through one of those subtle processes of mind common where the will is the principal agent in forming belief, General Washington's profanity strengthened the Colonel's faith.

He sat one day, for example, on a pile of rails binding up a wound with a handkerchief, when, in the road near him, Washington and Lee met, and that historical interview, when the warriors cursed each other like fishwives, occurred. "He was a

traitor, sir," said the Colonel, recounting the event, and referring
to Lee, "and deserved the curse God gave him through the
mouth of General Washington." The form of the anathema,
however, was not of the sort one would look for in Holy Writ.

After the war the Colonel settled upon the bank of the Ohio.
There he built himself a huge stone house, and for many years lived
in a gloomy sort of content, praying morning, noon, and night, and
when not looking after his farming interest, steadily reading his
Bible. He gave his pension to a Presbyterian parson and all his
time to the Lord.

Aunt Hetty was a house servant and a favorite of the old
Colonel, for while deeply religious, she differed from the other
servants in being very quiet in its expression. The master, a
taciturn man himself, seemed to recognize in this dignified, seldom-
speaking woman the sort of faith that moved his own soul. Per-
haps it was this gained for her more consideration than was
awarded the other slaves. No whip ever touched Aunt Hetty's
back. Even the overseer, a huge brute as an overseer was forced
to be, spoke to this strange woman in a respectful manner. The
old housekeeper had but one trouble, and that was her grandson,
the only living creature claiming kinship to her, and all the love
of the strong woman went out to this boy. He had white blood
in him and an exceedingly wayward nature. The real trouble
lay in the fact that the grandmother was so anxious to have this
pet of hers well trained that she over-trained him. The owner
had no need to interfere for the purpose of punishing the boy.
The whippings administered to the youth were so frequent and
severe that the Colonel's wife, in very pity, would, at times, interfere. When the lad ran away and spent a day in the woods, as he
did frequently, he was certain on his return to hang about the
premises until he could see his kind protector, and then run to
claim her interference.

The time came when this kind protector could be found no
longer about the sombre stone house. The stately old mother of
ten children passed away. With thin, matronly hands folded
across her meek breast, she was solemnly laid to rest with five of
her offspring, near the place, and the old Colonel found himself

alone, for the other five had grown up, married, and gone to make homes of their own.

The believer in Calvin and Calvin's God found it not good to be alone, and he called in the minister and elders to advise as to the propriety of his taking another partner to his house. The grave matter was, with much prayer, solemnly discussed, and the conclusion arrived at that it would be well for the old soldier to console his remaining days on earth with a suitable helpmate. Had the Colonel confided to this little council in the Lord the name of the woman he had selected, probably the council would not have been so unanimous. They thought, of course, that some staid elderly dame would be chosen, but the old man, like unto any other aged widower, saw to his liking a little girl scarcely out of her teens, and, with the recognized Biblical example of the Hebrew patriarchs before him, had authority for his choice.

The Widow Bentley, relict of the Hon. Richard Bentley, had come to the West with her only daughter to occupy the one piece of property the Hon. Virginian of Richmond had spared from his drinking and gambling to his family. They were very poor and very proud. The fall from the gay life of luxury at Richmond to the log-cabin on the Ohio, with all the privations of such a life, was hard on mother and daughter, so hard that when the Colonel, with dignified grace, offered himself as a husband to the little girl, it was a proposition to lift them from indigence to wealth again. There were tears shed over the consideration, but they were shed in private. The aged wooer saw only smiles as his offer was accepted.

The rude little church of God saw the sacrifice that the minister sanctified. The union of May and December received in this way the sanction of the border community, that, wild and rough in many respects, had a deep religious feeling of helpfulness lying under its rude structure, that saw in the old Colonel's choice only a special providence to the poor widow and orphan.

Both the recipients, however, awakened to the fact that the blessing was not an unmixed good. The same rigid economy that had marked the old soldier through life, the economy that made him live on the poor, uncertain pay of the Continental Army until a property, east of the mountains, left him by his father grew into a valuable estate, reigned in all its parsimony at his house. The widow and daughter looked want in the face from the door of their poor cabin, and privation followed them to the lonely stone mansion.

The worse feature, nevertheless, was found in Aunt Hetty. She had been for years housekeeper, and, during the widower-hood of her master, mistress of the mansion. Her good sense, and she had more of that than all the rest combined, would have dictated a quiet resignation of her post, but the Colonel regarded his new wife as a mere child—a fact, by the bye—and would listen to nothing of the sort. It was decreed that Aunt Hetty should continue to carry the keys and be responsible for the housekeeping. A rigid disciplinarian, his orders were law, and the poor mother, making a fierce fight for her daughter's rights, brought matters to a crisis that terminated the struggle. Aunt Hetty was disposed to yield to the young wife, but she conceived a fierce hatred for the widow. She went a little too far one day and gave the poor woman treatment that, from a negro, was insult. There is something in the subtle insolence of the slave that is maddening, and mother and daughter, in hot wrath, ordered Aunt Hetty to be whipped by the overseer.

Unfortunately this happened in the absence of the Colonel. The poor woman had so managed through her life of unrequited toil as to escape the lash. She submitted in silence. The overseer, who hated her, did his brutal business with a will, and the result was that Aunt Hetty was carried to her quarters insensible, and when her master returned he found her delirious from fever. From this delirium the old Colonel gathered an intimation of what had occurred. He brought forward the overseer, got the truth, and drove his respected mother-in-law from the house. He had the one grace to give her enough money to make her way to Richmond.

Aunt Hetty suffered in soul and body from the cruel torture to which she had been subjected, but her real danger came in the shape of a doctor, who bled, purged, and blistered the poor creature until there was scarcely any life left her. But her strong physique brought her through, and in a few weeks she returned to her duties as housekeeper. Whether the descendant of a kingly line or not, she had the true instincts of a slave, and, while she suffered keenly the punishment inflicted, she returned humbled to her work, and from that out tempered her service with a consideration for her young mistress never shown before. The poor wife got little comfort from this. The loss of her mother made life doubly miserable. The dreary monotony of the gloomy house fell upon her like a pall. She seemed buried alive, and the continuous religious exercises appeared to her prayers for the dead. Preachers, elders, and deacons came and went, and the stately old Colonel took no note of time in his meditations on eternity, and little of the so-called life save to keep a keen eye to the economical expenditures of the household.

The young wife looked up to her husband in fear. She heard his regular military step as he came with a shudder, and as he left with a sense of relief. While he was impressively polite, there was no tenderness in h's voice. no gentleness in his manner. He walked so much with God that he had no time for walks with his wife.

An event soon occurred that turned the wife's fear into positive aversion. One summer day there appeared a man at the mansion who seemed to bring the atmosphere and sunlight of another world to the sombre stone house. He came unexpectedly, for mails at that day were few and far between, and when Captain Philip Parnne walked in even the old Colonel, his uncle, gave a look of surprise. In his formal fashion he made the young man welcome as he presented him to his wife.

The wife saw before her as handsome a specimen of physical perfection as ever nature sat on end and endowed with human impulses. He had the Parnne features greatly improved. His dark eyes were larger and milder ; his Roman nose subdued to something less than an eagle's beak, while his marked ch'n made only a foundation to his well-formed head where the wealth of chestnut hair collected in a queue behind gave a grace unknown to his elders. Six feet in height, of spare figure, he balanced a pair of broad shoulders above his narrow hips with such ease that every movement was modulated and graceful.

Captain Phil. Parnne was on the best possible terms with himself and the world, for he was in superb health.   His courage, like
his stomach, was so perfect that he did not know that it existed.
He had, in consequence, no fears to consult and no favors to solicit.
Good natured from habit, he pleased his associates. who termed him
a good fellow without calling for any real kindness that would
have disturbed his comfort.   These surface readers would have
been astonished to learn that their good fellow was as selfish a man
as ever na ure created.   A close observer would have read in his
face the fact that he had all the selfishness Nature creates into iniquity so well defined that nothing but circumstances saved him
from being a recognized criminal.

It was the fashion of the day, got from the mother country,
where soldiers and statesmen were alike profligate, for our prominent men to be scoffers of religion and debauchees in social life.
Phil. Parnne partook of this condition.   He had many vices, all of
which were then consid red gentlemanly. and he had little principle and less conscience to offer any restraint.   His very visit to
his uncle's house and his stay there came of this lack of integrity.

Aaron Burr, with a few men on a raft, floating down the Ohio,
had alarmed the whole country.   We know now that this alarm
came from an affected anxiety on the part of Tom Jefferson, who
saw in the expedition an opportunity to rid himself of a dangerous
rival.   Be that as it might, Captain Phil. Parnne, U. S. A., was
sent in pursuit of the traitor.   Now it happened that Aaron Burr
was one of Captain Parnne's most intimate friends, and while he
(Phil.) kept himself clear of Burr's bold intrigues he was not inclined to make himself disagreeable.   To this end he tied his boat
to the shore, below his uncle's house, and quietly made a visit long
enough to enable Burr to escape the arrest the Government had
ordered.

The noble Captain expected to find the stay at his uncle's
house an unmitigated bore.   The sight of his youthful aunt brought
a change in that respect.   He saw before him a beautiful woman,
with a child like, trusting face, from whose deep blue eyes came a
sad, wistful expression that told of her unhappy life.   There are
some men who seem born without mothers, and bred to manhood

without sisters. Captain Phil. Parnne was of this sort, and from the first moment of his introduction he saw a means by which he could alleviate the monotony of his visit.

Another discovery dawned upon our Captain, that was that he bid fair to starve upon the meagre allowance of his uncle's table. To remedy this he not only brought up stores from the Government boat, but seizing his gun brought in from hunting enough to remedy the unpleasant deficit. He was returning from gunning one day, when he encountered his aunt on her way across the fields and through the woods to a friendly visit at a neighbor's. He turned and escorted her to her destination. Not only that, but under the plea that such excursions alone were dangerous, he learned the hour of her return and accompanied her home. These visits became singularly frequent, and as singularly delightful to both parties. While in the house the old Colonel was much given to religious disquisitions, to which the infidel nephew had to listen with profound attention. Away from this restraint the Captain and the fair wife gave free rein to merry talk that to her was simply delicious.

To all this the Colonel was blind. Not so, however, another pair of eyes that looked out from a shrewd, thoughtful mind. Aunt Hetty regarded the conduct of the two with great suspicion and no favor. She knew the wrong impending, but, strange to say, instead of moving to expose it, did all in her power to conceal it. To understand this it is necessary to know Aunt Hetty's motive. She fairly worshipped her master, and with her pride of family, so common to household slaves, would have submitted to any torture rather than have had any disgrace come to the house. It was not only the stain from which she shrank, but the pain and humiliation that would fall upon her idol, the Colonel.

If she had any doubt as to what had occurred, that doubt was solved by her grandson. who, still given to wild excursions came in one day out of breath and with stretched eyes, and tersely told to Aunt Hetty what he had seen. The revelation had scarcely fallen from his lips before Aunt Hetty, seizing him by the wool of his head, and shaking and pounding the poor boy until he was dazed, told him that if he ever dared utter such a lie again she would have the overseer whip him to death.

The autumn-time wore on and the forest livery of green was changing to the hectic hue that told of coming winter, when one still hazy afternoon of the Indian Summer the report of a mountain howitzer was heard up the river, and from the porch of the Colonel's house the family saw a boat—a broad-horn it was called—sweep round the bend. Upon the deck stood a group of officers, while the long oars were worked by soldiers. The b at was rounded to and tied immediately below the house, and three officers in full dress landed and ascended the long hill to the house.

Captain Phil. Parnne's self-granted leave of absence was at an end. Another army numbering sixty men was in pursuit of Aaron Burr. There was no excuse left for delaying immediate pursuit, and Captain Phil. felt no reluctance to moving, for he not only knew that his friend Burr was beyond pursuit, but was weary of a dalliance that had passed from smiles to tears. The poor woman had awakened from her guilty dream to a frightened consciousness of wrong that brought home to the handsome lover the fact that he was paying more for the gratification of his wicked passion than it had been worth. Fearing a scene at the last interview from her hysterical condition, he sought to have it in private. To this end, the day after the arrival of the troops, he shouldered his rifle and started for a last hunt, and she, understanding this, followed him under pretence of a visit.

They met in the wood but too well known to both, and immediately the poor creature threw herself with a piteous cry into the arms of her lover. He tried in vain to soothe and quiet her, and failing in this would have given more than he was worth to be rid of what he had so anxiously sought and obtained.

"Oh, take me with you, Philip," she wailed; "I shall die, I shall die."

"Come now, little one," he cried, "don't be silly. I cannot take you, not now at least, but I will return in a few weeks and then—"

Captain Phil. paused suddenly and threw the woman from him so quickly, and with such violence, that she fel with a cry. He had happened to look up, and saw in the oak immediately above him a pair of bright eyes that belonged to the half-hidden figure of Aunt Hetty's grandson. Seizing his rifle that he had leaned against the trunk of the tree he brought it to his shoulder. The poor woman, taking in the situation at a glance, sprung to her feet and caught her lover's arm as she cried :

" Oh, don't, Phil., for God's sake, don't."

He lowered the gun.

" Come down, you scoundrel, come down."

The boy slid to the ground and stood trembling before the two.

" Now go on to your visit," he continued to the woman.

" But you won't hurt him, Phil ? "

" That depends on his hurting us, but you must hurry," and seeing her hesitation he added to the boy : " Get home, you damned idiot, get home."

Satisfied with this, the two, mistress and slave, started in opposite directions.

The path on which Captain Parnne stood ran straight in view to him for nearly a hundred yards. He was not, however, at the centre. The woman had the shorter space to travel before reaching the turn, but she staggered on slowly. The boy had the longer distance, but he almost ran.

The Captain, gun in hand, watched his love. He saw her disappear behind the bushes, and turned in time to see the boy just at the end of the path. Throwing up his rifle, he fired instantly. The whip-like report rang out, a slender stream of smoke spurted from the muzzle, and the poor boy, throwing up his arms, without a cry, seemed to leap into the gully ahead, from which the path turned to the right.

The Captain walked to the point where the woman had disappeared and saw her yet wending her way. Then he returned and looked down the ravine into which the murdered boy had fallen. He saw the body hanging across a bent sapling. Descending the steep declivity, holding to shrubs and roots, he removed all traces of the fall. Then pulling the body from over the bending sapling, muttered " That will do," and continued his hunt.

Some hours afterwards, returning to the house, our Captain

coolly informed his uncle that he had accidentally shot one of his negroes.

The old soldier gazed at him from under his shaggy eyebrows and said :

" How could that happen?"

" Stupidly enough. I heard a breaking of brush in a ravine below me, and thinking it a deer, fired at the object I indistinctly saw, and killed that boy whose life seemed to be spent in larking through the woods."

"Yes," said the Colonel, "and I expected him to come to such an end ; where is the body?"

"If you will give me a couple of men I will show them," said the Captain, and the order was given.

Aunt Hetty had heard all this ; a shudder passed through her frame, and a sharp glance came from her keen eyes, but she said nothing. Clamping her teeth together, she even gave the order for the improvised pall bearers. What agony the poor creature suffered was never known, for she never gave it sound. When the limp remains of all she had on earth was carried in, her grief was either under too strong control or too deep for tears. She neither wept nor wrung her poor labor-hardened hands—those humble, motherly hands that had caressed and punished this sole recipient of all her love and care. There was a look in her eyes, however, that, had the Captain noticed, would at least have made him feel uneasy.

Under the Colonel's orders, the body was laid on sheet-covered boards in the hall until a coffin could be procured and a minister brought to render the last rites to the dead.

The Captain had his luggage carried to the boat without waiting for his aunt's return to take his leave. It was late when she came. As Mrs. Parnne left the Captain, it happened that the wind was blowing from her towards the fatal spot, so that she did not hear the crack of the rifle that did the fatal work. She was only troubled by the thought of the exposure that might follow the boy's return. Anxious about this and this alone, she lingered at the neighbor's until the last moment, and then returned in ignorance of what had occurred.

The sun was sinking in the hazy west, and shadows had gathered in that gloomy hall when she entered. She gave one look at the dead, and then, without a sound, fell to the floor.

Aunt Hetty would have warned her had she dreamed that the guilty wife was unaware of the murder. Her keen sense had comprehended the situation, but she had included one too many in the crime. As it was, she hastily seized her mistress in her arms and dragged her to her bedroom.

"Hush, missus, for God's sake, hush," she cried, as the poor woman, after much rubbing, returned wailing to consciousness. "Don't say dem words, de mars'll heah you shriek."

As her admonitions had no effect, she hastily opened the Colonel's medicine-chest, and grasping the laudanum, poured a heavy dose down the throat of her mistress. When the old Colonel looked in not long after, he found his wife sleeping like an infant. But Aunt Hetty watched her all the night through all the same. Between the dead boy in the hall and her sick mistress in the room, that stern nature counted the hours until near midnight, when her mistress awoke too exhausted to cry out.

"Go to him," she gasped, "tell him I am dying, and that with my last breath I pardon and bless him."

Captain Parnne and his companions were having a carouse on the boat. A table had been spread in the rude cabin, and with an abundance of game, and yet more of liquor, the midnight came upon them all more or less drunk. The noisiest one was the Captain, who laughed and talked and sang incessantly. It was the day when such feasts were garnished with songs, in which the landlord was admonished to "fill the flowing bowl" that they might "drink to the lass," and our Captain had a rich, mellow voice with which to roll out the stupid numbers.

Did the Captain seek to drown the voices of the dead and dying, that a little way from him were speaking, speaking as if they never would be still. Let that be as it may, he was startled when his sergeant touched him on the shoulder and told him that a woman on the bank wanted to see him. He followed the man out across the plank and ascended the steep bank as directed.

The moon at the full cast a light on wood and river, which

would have been that of day but for the fog that floated on the cool autumnal air along the stream. While the wooded bluffs above were clear and well-defined against the sky, below and about him the white vapor made an inland sea almost as dense to the eye as the waters of the Ohio. Captain Parnne found himself in the presence of Aunt Hetty.

"Well, Aunty," he said, "what is it now?" She straightened herself up in the misty moonlight, appearing far taller in the dim light, and said in a voice in which anguish seemed held at the throat by a stern resolve:

"Captain Phil. Parnne, I come to ye wid de blessin' ob de guilty, and de cuss of de innercent. De woman ye has ruined is a dyin', and de blood of my poor boy cries to God from de ground foh veng-ance. I cuss ye, I cuss ye! May ye walk in trouble all yo days, and when ye dies may death come to ye wid de woe ob hell befo' ye feels it. De mark ob Cain is on yo fo'head. Tak de blessin' of de wicked an de cuss ob de innercent."

"Oh, go to hell, you old hag!" roared the Captain, as the tall form of the terrible woman seemed to melt from him in the mist of the river.

Propped on pillows poor Mrs. Parnne gazed through the window with wistful eyes upon the river far below. The beautiful stream, framed in by the golden foliage of autumn, offered to her sight a long stretch in the mellow sunlight. Boats appeared at long intervals, floated by and disappeared, but no flag waved above any one of them; no roll of drum or clear bugle-call told of what she longed with aching heart-hunger to see. The river had swept all that from her life—a frail woe-stricken life, that erelong floated out on that mightier river of death into the vast unknown. She was given sweet Christian burial. The minister dwelt upon her many virtues and chaste womanly life, and a text of Scripture indicating the same was duly inscribed upon her tomb. The real story, the terrible truth, lay locked in Aunt Hetty's heart, nor would it have ever been known, but for a revelation made to a brother officer by Captain Philip during a carouse. It reached the ears of many of the family, but never those of the widower. The old Colonel died lamenting the loss of his young spouse, and to-day the mouldering bones lie buried between those of the two wives, and upon the moss-covered headstones one may read of pious and chaste lives ; but no monument. humble or pretentious, tells of the one heroic life of the poor slave, who carried to her narrow grave the silent agony of her grief and pride.

MR. BARDOLPH BOTTLES.

THE Hon. Bardolph Bottles—I call him that because that is not his name—is a gentleman—and I call him so because it is polite—of stout body, florid complexion, with the little mind he possesses spread all over him.

By this I mean that the Hon. Bottles has his character and force thereof more in his temperament than in his development of brain. All men of action are more or less of this sort. All men of thought are the reverse. That is, thought begets caution and distrust in one. The absence of thought gives place to confidence and quick action, which satisfies the masses, and makes the prompt, conceited man a leader of men.

If the last named is lucky, and he is apt to be, and is solemn enough, he wins a monument. "All the great monuments of earth were built to solemn asses," said the witty and eloquent Tom Corwin.

Now, Bottles is not solemn, and therefore will miss his monument. But Bottles does not want a monument. He can tell you that he does not want a monument ; if he did he would buy one, for Bottles is a millionaire. He would rather use his money in the purchase of Congressmen, salting of mines, organizing construction companies for the building of railroads, and other processes of an ingenious sort, through which money may be accumulated.

"Monuments, sir? What the blank do I want with a monument? Monuments don't pay. What is it to old George that he has a smoke-stack six hundred feet high ? They call that a monument. I suppose it is. It is certainly not anything else. I wouldn't give three dollars and thirty-seven and a half cents for it. Might use it for advertising purposes. Wouldn't be a bad dodge," and the Honorable Bottles will laugh until his round face gets redder than ordinary.

My hero began active life when quite young. as a stable boy. He picked up his reading and writing as he did old clothes, and worn hats and toeless shoes. As for arithmetic, it came to him, as Dogberry asserted of the kindred branches, by nature, but he did not thank God for it, any more than he did for his fat nose and cunning disposition.

He developed into a jockey, and rode racers to win or lose, as he was paid to win or lose. When grown too heavy for this, he bought the stock of a failing liquor dealer. He opened a lager-beer saloon at the entrance of a camp-meeting ground. The pious men who established this camp of the Lord in the wilderness of sin could prohibit the sale of alcoholic liquors within a mile of their tents, but there was some sort of a mystery about beer that baffled all their efforts. They were forced to buy out Bottles, on his own terms, and Bottles was pleased with the transaction.

Bardolph used his money to purchase a billiard-room, and, back of this room, opened a gambling resort. The young men entering the gilded saloon for a game of billiards were invited back to a supper, and when well stimulated with liquor were robbed under a show of gambling. A few defalcations, several thefts by clerks, and at last a suicide upon the premises, made the business "too hot for him," as Bottles expressed it, and he sold the billiard-room and abandoned the place. The war breaking out about this time, Bottles, full of patriotic enthusiasm, joined the army as a sutler. This was Bottles' worst speculation, owing to the sudden and continuous retreats of our armies that occurred, although we have quite forgotten the fact, during the first two years of the war, "profits did not accrue." On the contrary, Bottles was so reduced in pocket that he was forced to ask for, and secured, a commission in the army.

Now, Bardolph, unlike the warrior I have named him after, is a plucky fellow, and he fought his men at all hours, on all occasions, and rose rapidly in rank. One day, when the shoeless, shirtless, half starved host of rebels, under Lee, were falling back. leaving behind them a highway of dead and dying, Bottles made one of his impetuous rushes, and got hurt by the dying tiger. A shot through his shoulder lifted Bottles from his saddle, and twenty soldiers carried him off the field, with that tender solicitude always shown by men going to the war toward a wounded comrade.

As our hero had no limbs to amputate nor a wound that would justify any sort of surgical operation, he was left for the good Sisters of Charity to nurse into life.

The care given Bottles by the pious sisters had a religious influence on the man. He will to this day knock a man down who dares to say aught against the Catholic Church, and he will swear the most awful oaths to strengthen his eulogy, often uttered, of the patient angels who nursed him while wounded.

While lying between life and death Bottles had time to gravely consider his condition, and, with pious determination, resolved to give up soldiering and turn his attention to cotton.

As soon as he "got on end," to use his own phraseology, he bade the sisters a tender adieu, and, working his way to Washington, solicited and obtained from Secretary Chase a permit to trade beyond our lines in cotton. He was a gallant soldier, decorated with an ugly wound, and had a right, therefore, to privileges.

It was Bottles' great opportunity, and he seized it with avidity. His experience as a sutler, and a soldier, added to his audacity, made him take risks his brother dealers in cotton shrank from. He found it much easier to pierce our lines with cotton than he had the enemy's lines with bayonets. He came out of the business with over two hundred thousand dollars in bank.

After Lee's surrender he was assigned to duty, at his own request, in the Freedman's Bureau, and was sent South. From that part of our great country he returned a United States Senator. He served two terms in that solemn body, but was found ineligible for a third, owing to a lien being developed by the penitentiary, from certain transactions in bonds that the State he was supposed to represent considered fraudulent. How he escaped the scandal of even a trial I never learned.

Retiring from the Senate, Bardolph soon appeared as a railroad operator at the South. The railroads of that region having been almost destroyed by the war, my hero used his short means in buying up, for a mere song, the more important lines, and, associating with himself certain prominent Confederates, went to reconstructing, well knowing that as the South recovered from her prostration these lines would be of immense value.

Had the business been pursued honestly no one could question the right to the money accumulated by the promoters. But honesty was a quality Bottles knew little of, and cared less. He took the prominent Southerners in with him, as a guard against investigation of his bond business, and to give color and popularity to his ventures. It was not long, however, before these associates discovered that Bottles was making an unfair divide, and war broke out. These associates were not the sort of men to trifle with, but Bottles was their equal in that respect, and would have fought it out, probably to a success, but for a little transaction that had occurred when Bottles was Senator and yet dealing in fraudulent bonds.

Once upon a time there existed in Wall Street a couple of female brokers. They were lovely to look upon, and while wise as serpents were innocent as doves—soiled doves. Bottles, like all of us, has his weaknesses, and the elder of the lovely brokers proved one of them. To his eyes she was "as pretty as a painted wagon or a Missouri mule," to use his own comparisons, and he was fool enough, while in New York seeking to conceal his bonds, to employ these women. It was during an entertainment at their gorgeously furnished house, after my hero had probably imbibed too much champagne.

Be that as it may, some time after, when sick of his brokers, he had a settlement. One item in their account was $10,000. He swore with a great oath, that he would allow no such swindle, and a quarrel followed that cost him twenty times the $10,000 charged.

These gifted and gentle brokers were cats, that could sit at a hole quietly a long time, for an opportunity to steal out.

The opportunity appeared when Bottles quarrelled with his Southern associates. The gentle brokers were quick to sell their information, and his wronged brother railroaders were able to fetch the penitentiary again to the gaze of Bottles, and so force him out of the enterprise.

Life is a campaign, not a battle, and has its defeats as well as its victories. Bardolph was defeated, but not destroyed, and he next turned his attention, as a great financial operator, to railroads being built, at the West, on appropriations of money and land grants from the Government.

Entering this great national enterprise, the ingenious mind of Bottles suggested a plan through which the great national thorough-fare could be built by the Government, and owned by the company. Organizing this last named, he immediately proceeded to create a construction company out of the railroad company itself, and then contracted for the construction. As the two companies consisted of the same men, the contracts were extremely liberal, so that the great national throughfare was made to cost twice the amount necessary to build it, and after an expenditure of appro-priations in making the road, those ingenious gentlemen, who had not expended a cent, issued to themselves evidences of indebted-ness, some of which were distributed through Congress where it was supposed "they would do the most good."

The members caught holding this stock were investigated and severely censured, but the men who succeeded in stealing some eighty millions are yet unpunished, my hero, Bottles, among the rest.

I was travelling West some years since, when the Honorable Bottles invaded the sleeper I helped fill. Time, like Justice, had dealt gently with the sutler, soldier, statesman, and r ilroad king. The snow of years was sprinkling the little hair and profuse beard left him. His waist had become traditionary, and his legs more slender than of old, but his form was yet erect, his movements act-ive, his voice strong and hearty, and his eyes bright as ever. He greeted me with a hearty shake and a merry laugh, as he directed and aided in distributing his luggage.

He had, among other things, a huge lunch-basket and a case of champagne. As the day promised to be exceedingly hot, for it was in midsummer, he directed the conductor of the sleeper to take the bottles from the basket quietly and drop them in the ice-cooler of the car.

"Why, General," I said, "you surely are not going to put those dirty bottles in the water the passengers have to drink?"

"Oh, Tom can wipe them off. Wipe 'em off, Tom. That's all right."

Tom left to execute this extraordinary order, and soon the General and I were deep in reminiscences of the past, for I had known him for fourteen years, in and about the national capital, and always found him exceedingly entertaining.

As time wore on that morning I observed that the passengers of our sleeper were exceedingly thirsty and resorted continually to the cooler for water. I further observed, after a time, that the women and children had flushed faces and brightened eyes, and that, after a time, they grew noisy. An old lady, weighing some two hundred, after a vain attempt to look at the end of her nose, settled back into a sleep, with her head thrown back, that opened her mouth, and not only started a heavy article of snore but dropped a very fair article of "store teeth" in her lap. Four young men, evidently commercial travellers, engaged in a game of poker, grew loudly hilarious at first, then got quarrelsome, and at last drew revolvers and were disarmed by the conductor and brakeman, amid shrieks of the women that were unusually loud.

"Well," said Bottles, "this is the crankiest car I ever boarded. What the blank is the matter with them anyhow?"

The mystery was solved about noon. Bottles opened his lunch-basket, and made a spread of cold quails, pickles, *paté de foie gras* and other costly delicacies. and then sent the porter for a bottle of champagne. The man returned, looking as if he had seen the ghost of Guiteau.

"General," he said in a stage whisper, "dere ain't no champagne, sah."

"Why, what's gone with it?"

"Well. you see, sah, de motion ob de cah, or ice, in de coolahs, hab done broke all de bottles, and dese or'nary people has been drinkin' youah champagne all mawnin', sah."

"Well, I be damned," said the Honorable Bottles.

ABOUT LOVE AND LAW.

" I TELL you, young gentlemen, that I once enjoyed this sort of thing probably more than you do. When a young man I was very much of a young man. I was impulsive, propulsive, sentimental—in fact, considerably troubled with the fool."

The Judge leaned back in his arm-chair, and, looking at his handsome and rather hard face, it was difficult to believe, even seen through a cloud of cigar smoke and a glass of champagne at his elbow, that the Judge had ever been troubled with a weakness of any sort. Standing at the head of his profession, he was noted not only for his brilliant qualities, but his steady, unremitting hard work. The speech I have put to record was made after a bar supper, when a few young men gathered around him in a cosey sitting-room to enjoy his sharp utterances and witty remarks.

" Come, Judge, tell us about yourself at that mythical age you speak of."

" Well, young gentlemen, I was admitted to the bar at the town of Herat, in New England. To tell you the truth, I made the closest shave ever accomplished by an idle student. Admitting me to the bar under the circumstances was simply ridiculous. I owed my success to old Judge Colville, the chairman of the committee, who said to his associates, after they had got through the fatiguing process of finding how little I knew. 'Gentlemen, we have admitted a good deal of information, with little ability, and I want now to admit one possessed of much ability and no information.' The whimsical proposition took and I was duly commissioned attorney at law and solicitor in chancery.

" The reason for this ridiculous exhibition was in the fact that for nearly a year previous I had been devoting myself to a little widow instead of the law. I had collided on a sweet creature of a blond make, relict of a departed music-master, who, dying, had left his charming widow sole possessor of an old piano, worn-out music-stool, and the name of Mrs. De Wiggles. She had what the world would pronounce a baby face, but to me it was that of an angel. She had large, dreamy blue eyes, fluffy light hair, rosy round cheeks, and a mouth so perfect that when her lips opened and displayed the regular little ivory teeth it appeared the pearly gate of paradise. Her father was minster of a fashionable church and she sang in the choir. She had a shy, and yet frank, way with her that played old Satan with all the students of Herat.

"I fell madly in love with the little widow and sold my gun to purchase a guitar. When not clawing at this vile instrument, I was dancing attendance on my love, escorting her to church, for I became extremely devout, praying earnestly to the little cherub that sat up aloft—that is in the choir—going to lectures, pious picnics; and when not thus engaged I put in my time writing love-songs and howling them out by moonlight under her window.

"The little creature favored my suit and we were engaged, with an understanding that the marriage was not to come off until after my admission to the bar, when a practice would enable me to support my divinity.

"I nearly ruined myself in the purchase of an engagement-ring for her. It was a sweet little thing, made up of a serpent with its tail in its mouth, to indicate eternity, and clustered with pearls, having two little diamonds for eyes.

"After securing my prize I sat down to hard work. It was too late. The law is a jealous mistress, young gentlemen, and is especially hostile to blue eyes, fluffy hair, and a pearly gate to paradise. I toiled on in a vain endeavor to make up for lost time, and got through, as I tell you, on the whim of an eccentric old gentleman.

"To open an office and make a bid for business followed, of course. On the score of economy I made my office and bedroom one. I had a folding couch that I made up myself every morning into the form of a wardrobe. At least this was the delusion I indulged in. It had an aggravating way, after it had been set on end, of escaping the spring and coming down with a bang most decidedly offensive. I think the bugs used to start that spring, otherwise it must have been Satan himself, for it came down one day on the only client that ever ventured into my den.

" She was a feeble old lady, and suffered so from the dead-fall that I had to support her for weeks at the hospital.

" This bed, when a bed, stood across a door that led into a vacant room back of my office. I give you these particulars, young gentlemen, because they are necessary for a better understanding of the ex raordinary case that followed.

" The course of true love never does run smooth, and mine got into the rapids caused by a fat hatter before it took its tumble over the precipice where it disappeared forever. This hatter, who answered to the name of Amity Dodd, was an acquaintance of mine, and a creditor, for I not only owed him for hats and caps, but I had borrowed of him divers sums of money. He was a good-natured clam on legs, with a bulbous termination to his back-bone which resembled a pumpkin. He always reminded me of the two lines in the old ballad which said :

> His head being larger than common,
> O'erbalanced the rest of his fat.

" Amity Dodd played upon the flute. I never knew a clam on end but what did play upon the flute. And, being thus musically inclined, took it into his bulbous adipose that he would like well to be acquainted with the widow, De Wiggles, and so he asked me to introduce him. I could not well refuse on account of those bills. I asked permission of my love, telling her at the same time that he was a poor sort of a creature, but played divinely on the flute and sold hats at a great profit.

" Amity Dodd was introduced. Amity Dodd got to be very intimate. At first his flute and my guitar, the widow's piano, and sweet voices made up little concerts that caused the neighbors to wish they were dead. After a time my guitar was dropped out, and the concerts went on without me. Then the hatter got to be sort of an escort at church, concerts, lectures, and when I remonstrated my little intended wife would laugh like a child and say, 'Poor fat man, I feel so sorry for him.'

"One fatal afternoon I called unexpectedly upon my love, and entering the parlor unannounced, as was customary, I found my love in the arms of my hatter.

"I was jilted, betrayed. I felt myself destroyed and left the house in a frenzy of madness which expressed itself with a slam of the front door that broke the hinges, knocked out a panel, and made the paternal author of the fair De Wiggles bounce out of his chair under the impression that an earthquake had struck that part of the town.

"Ah, me, what days and nights of desolation's nakedness followed that awful betrayal of my youthful affections. I fled the town, lived in a gloomy way at a country farm-house on heavy bread, sour milk, and soul-destroying fried bacon. When at last resolved into a cynical, Byronic, cut-my-throat-at-midnight sort of character I returned to find that the faithless De Wiggles was converted into Mrs. Amity Dodd. I tell you, young gentlemen, that those scornful words wrought into the poetry of 'Locksley Hall' by Lord Tennyson were milk and water to the feelings of a young man who finds his love captured and carried off by a low hatter who plays the flute.

"I survived, however, and gradually returned to my ordinary food and sleep. This sleep returned to me slowly, and many a night I found it extremely difficult to escape a sense of my misfortune and the music of the mosquitoes. One night I had dropped into a profound sleep, and dreaming that I had converted the miserable hatter into an old smooth-bore and was firing him at the perfidious widow, I was suddenly awakened by some one falling upon me. Throwing up my arms instinctively, I seized a man just as a revolver exploded in the room. Clutching the intruder firmly by the throat, I found myself dragged into the vacant room back of my office. Here a fierce tussle occurred, my assailant evidently trying to escape me, while I instinctively held to him. He succeeded, however, in escaping out of my grasp through an open window to a roof beyond, and as he clattered down I heard a shout, a shot, and then came a dead silence in the bright moonlight of the summer night. I returned to my office and bedroom, struck a light, and found a revolver, with one chamber exploded, lying upon the floor. The next day's papers told of a burglary that had been committed upon the residence of the Rev. Mr. Timmins, in which certain valuables belonging to Mrs. Amity Dodd had been abstracted. The papers went on to say that the thief had been captured after a chase over roofs, and the valuables taken found upon his person.

"I laughed a scornful laugh at this circumstance, and had dismissed it from my mind, when, one day, entering my office after breakfast, I found the engagement-ring I had given my late *fiancée*, now Mrs. Am ty Dodd.

"I called up the old Irishwoman and asked where this article came from. 'Shure,' she said, 'I found it on the floor, and put it on your table.' I thought. of course, the fickle woman had been taken with sudden compunction and returned me my poor ring.

"At the next term of court the burglar of the Dodd apartment was arraigned, with other prisoners, and having told the court he was too poor to employ an attorney, Judge Colville turned to a friend of mine, Brock Harrison, who had just been admitted to the bar, and said : 'Brother Harrison, take this prisoner and see him legally convicted.'

"A sudden impulse seized me, and I volunteered to assist. There wasn't the ghost of a chance for the fellow's acquittal. He had been seen to enter the house, and when the alarm was given and the police rallied he was observed stealing out. He escaped over some roofs, and for a moment seemed to have got free when the report of a pistol attracted attention and the thief was caught coming from my room with the missing valuables upon his person. His stumbling over my bed, dropping his revolver that exploded as it struck the floor, proved his ruin. I don't know why I did such an insane thing as to interfere in this trial. But I knew that my late love had to be the prosecuting witness, and a morbid desire to face her, question her, and put her down with my lofty indifference, took possession of me.

"On the day of the trial the court-house was crowded, and all the congregation of the Rev. Mr Timmins made it a point to attend. The trial began, and after the police had told how they caught and captured the thief, Mrs. Amity Dodd was called to the stand. My heart for a second stood still as she lifted her little hand to be sworn. I mastered my emotions to see that she appeared prettier than ever, and she was just as shy, yet frank and winning, as at any period of her treacherous life. At the request of the prosecutor she told the story of the robbery. When through, the State turned her over to me for a cross-examination, and I set myself to the task. A dead silence pervaded the court-room. In a low, steady voice I said : 'Madam, will you please tell the court what those articles were that were taken on the night of the robbery ?' She went over the list, and among the rest described my ring. 'Madam, I said, do you mean to assert that this ring was among the articles taken that night ?' and I took the little jewel from my vest-pocket and held it before her. She faltered, hesitated, and then answered : 'Yes.' 'Is it your property ?' I asked. She answered in a low tone : 'Yes.' 'Was it purchased by you ?' I asked. The court could just hear the word 'gift' gasped out. 'Given you by whom ?' I asked. Mrs. Amity Dodd faltered out something and fell over in a dead faint.

"'What is the meaning of this examination ?' demanded the little dried-up prosecutor.

"'We were about to ask the same question,' said the Court.

"'Nothing.' I replied, 'only to show that the prosecuting witness has a very unreliable memory. The ring, as we are prepared to show, has been in our possession for some time and could not, therefore, have been among the articles stolen at night.'

"'Hold on, Bob,' whispered Brock to me, 'you are driving into trouble. Our fellow tells me he did steal that ring.'

"'He lies,' I retorted, 'I gave her that ring, and she returned it to me.'

"'Well,' remarked the court, 'the point is immaterial ; there seems to be enough of yellow jewelry to make this grand larceny. Proceed with the case.' Brock and the prosecutor declined arguing. Brock told me in an undertone that we hadn't a leg to stand on. I became possessed of a devil, and occupied half an hour in addressing the jury on the unreliability of testimony offered by women, children, idiots, and policemen. I was exceedingly sarcastic on females in general, and I stuck that ring under the nose of the prosecutor, flourished it in the eyes of the jury, until the ring got to be the most prominent feature of the case. The sensation created by the fainting of the prosecuting witness was continued till the close of my extraordinary speech.

"The prosecutor, a specimen Yankee run to seed, sat grim and silent, and when he arose to reply had in his grim countenance an expression of dry humor that soon found vent in words that were first followed by smiles and then roars of laughter on the part of the court-room. He began by telling of my love affair, how I was led on and then jilted, and he drew a pathetic picture of my blighted affections. He told how a villain of a hatter had wound himself around the heart of the fair widow and crowded me out into a cold, unfeeling world. He said, of course the hatter made himself felt, and all true maidens and gallant swains were bound to feel for me. He felt for me himself, for he had been in love, had been disappointed and stunted in his growth, and had never developed into the handsome manhood once promised him.

"All this was uttered in the deepest solemnity and most earnest manner. When a roar of laughter greeted him he would turn and look upon the crowd, with an expression of amazement, which seemed to say, 'Why this unseemly levity?'

"This would be followed by yet more boisterous merriment, lasting sometimes for a moment or more.

"The crowning outrage of this wretch came in on his theory of defence. He claimed that, driven to madness by my wrongs, I had employed this villain of a burglar to break into the hatter's matrimonial bower and abstract the token of my affection, which the fair widow, now the wife of the skilled artisan in headgear, had failed or refused to return.

"'Why, gentlemen,' he cried, 'the burglar made a bee-line from the bower across the house tops to the bedroom and office of his employer, this blighted being, and then left this token of former bliss in the hands of this melancholy man. That the low-born villain, without a particle of romance in his soul, undertook to do a little business on his own account, abstracting the hatter's watch, a silver time-piece of great value as a family heir-loom, the madam's hair-pins, and other valuables, is not to be wondered at. It is to be be deplored that a beautiful little ro-mance was destroyed by this low-born villain of a burglar.'

"How I got from the court-room to my office I do not know. My self-possession, indeed, my mind, as the Pennsylvanian remarked at the battle of Gettysburg, was 'all tore up.' I had scarcely time to remove my hat when the place was invaded by the indignant hatter. He was accompanied by his foreman, a limestone forma-tion, tinctured in blue and black by the dyes he handled.

"'You have insulted my wife,' cried the hatter, putting his unpleasant countenance near mine.

"'Of course I have,' I roared insanely, 'and I am glad of it. She will find now what it is to lack the protection of a man.,

"'Hit him, boss,' exclaimed the foreman, with that self-com-posed manner always peculiar to the man who goes along as a friend. The indignant hatter lifted his arms, raising his pudgy fist as high above his head as he could, intending to bring it down upon me with great force.

"I had not studied the noble art of self-defence for nothing, and I struck my entire weight from the shoulder into his intel-lectual countenance, that, encountering his nose, his only guard, knocked that member, having struck it, flat, and sent the hat-building, flute-playing enemy prone upon the floor. The foreman first picked up the hat of h's boss, and then the boss himself. While holding him in his arms, I proceeded to paint his intellect-ual outlook a deep red.

"'Stop that!' cried the foreman, and as I did not obey, he struck at me, and I proceeded at once to give him the benefit of a paper-weight that brought the entire establishment to the floor. Rushing out to the street, with a bang of the door behind me, which had upon it a placard notifying my supposed clients that I had gone to dinner and would be back in twenty minutes, I unfortunately encountered the prosecuting attorney. He was returning from the court accompanied by two other lawyers. They were in a most hilarious mood, laughing, doubtlessly, over the late trial. This was too much for me, and, rushing at the humorous legal luminary, I slapped his mouth ; his comical expression of utter amazement and fright on this occasion was genuine. Dropping his green bag, he turned to fly. As his rear elevation presented itself to me, I administered a kick that seemed to lift him from the pavement and so accelerated his flight that he disappeared like magic in a tin-shop near us.

"That night I was surrounded by a gang of students singing a refrain, part of which, as I remember it, ran something like this:

> When first I lost my little rose,
> I eased my aching heart with blows
> And hit the hatter on the nose, O M'riar !

"The O M'riar went off into cat yells of the most exasperating character.

"The journals next day were full of me. In some I was treated of as an idiot ; in others as an assassin and thief.

"I should have been driven into an asylum for lunatics had it not been for my old friend, Judge Colville, who came to see me.

"'You have got yourself into a pretty mess, my boy,' he said, 'and the best thing you can do is to vacate this town and go West.'

"I replied humbly that I would be glad to do so had I the means. He volunteered to loan me a hundred dollars, and that night I left the town of Herat never to see it again."

OLD SHACK.

It was Josh Billings, I believe, who called our attention to the fact that monkeys and negroes were born old. A young monkey and a negro baby have an expression of vast experience from the first stage. It does not change as the years roll by. A negro retires from active life at about forty years of age, and at sixty tacks on a hundred years and becomes one of Washington's body-servants. There is nothing in his appearance that contradicts this assumption. On the contrary, his wrinkled solemnity and words of worldly wisdom go far to confirm his assumption.

I never knew how old the venerable Shack was. He claimed to have been my grandfather's body-servant during the Revolution and through the war of '12. He could have been this and not reached over a hundred when he appeared at Macochee at the head of about twenty colored men, women, and children, escaped slaves from my grandfather's farm, Federal Hall, Boone County, Kentucky. My father was perfectly amazed at their appearance, for slavery at Federal Hall, as he remembered it, was purely nominal. The negroes worked when they felt like it, which was very seldom ; and, owing to the disappearance of fences, crops had come to be traditional. When Shack was remonstrated with for his ungrateful conduct he replied :

"I'ze got as high regard for de ole Kurnel as I'ze got for Gineral Washington hisself. But you see, young Mass' Saunders comes up and is mi'ty handy wit de whip. We goes up to the ole Kurnel to 'monstrate, and de ole Kurnel says, says he : 'You is a lot ob or'nary niggers. You is,' says he, 'a burden and a nuisance,' says he. 'I wish you'd jes' clar out.' Dat talk ob de ole Kurnel jes' brought de tears to my eyes, foh you see I'd been wit' him troo all de big wahs. I nu's him when he was sick, I

nu's him when he was wounded ; I served him like intelligent
nigger all the time, and to hav' him use dem language hurt de ole
niggers' feelin's.   So we jes' up and said, ' Good by, massah, we's
goin'.   De ole massah's mighty pious man ; but, my sole, but he
did use some mighty profane langwidge.   Den we all lifted up
our Ebinezers and wept.   Den de ole man took his big stick wid
de gold head, which his regimen' gib him, and he jest drove us
niggers out.   I don't think, Massah Ben, dat ole Massah Kurnel
is in his proppah mind."

However indignant the old Colonel might have been to see his
slaves leave in broad daylight, he made no effort to reclaim them.
On the contrary, when my father wrote him that his negroes were
at Macochee, and wished to know what he should do about it, he
replied by post, in a letter that cost twenty-five cents, that he felt
very much relieved at their going, and hoped steps might be taken
to prevent their return, especially that old rascal Shack, who had
been at the bottom and cause of all the laziness, lying, and theft of
the gang.

To understand and appreciate this it is only necessary to know
that the old Colonel, like many of the more conscientious first
settlers of Kentucky, was at heart an Abolitionist.   His soul re-
volted at the thought of unrequited toil on the part of these poor
creatures.   He had attempted to treat them as free laborers, and
failed in the most ignominious manner.

The escaped slaves scattered and disappeared, all save old
Shack, who stuck to Macochee the rest of his days.

He persisted in going through the forms of work, sometimes
to the vexation of my father, but generally to the amusement of
all the family.   As the body-servant of the old Colonel through
two wars, it was entertaining to note his sense of superiority over
all of us, and the care he felt for the old Colonel's dignity and
reputation.   The old gentleman used to relate that there was but
one occasion when Shack forgot himself and the respect due his
master.   That event happened when in full retreat, on horseback, from the Indians, after a frightful defeat and massacre.
The two came upon a swamp.   The Colonel, reining up his steed,
turned to Shack and said :

"Well, Shack, what shall we do here?"

"Lor bress you, massah, dis no place to conversate!" cried the poor negro, driving past his master and plunging into the swamp, for in the distance he heard the yells of the pursuing red men.

Fortunately, the Indians missed their trail and went off to the left, leaving the Colonel to pull his servant out of the quagmire.

Much of my boyish entertainment consisted in tricks played upon old Shack. He was extremely superstitious, and generally attributed my doings to the active interference of Satan.

I remember once coming upon Shack in a deep snow, engaged in hauling a sled-load of hickory fuel from the woods to the house. He was riding one of the horses while leading the other, and so engaged with the team that he passed without seeing me. I ran after and got upon the load and then went to work throwing it off, a stick at a time, without his knowledge, until all was gone, when I jumped off and saw the old man pull the empty sled solemnly into the wood-house. A moment after I came upon the scene and saw Shack regarding his empty sled with a ludicrous expression of amazement no words can describe.

"What's the matter, Shack?" I asked, with assumed innocence.

"I dunno," he responded, scratching his gray wool, while great beads of perspiration started from his frightened countenance. "You see, I started from Hickory Hollow wid a big load, an' jess see you'self. I gits here widout a stick."

"You old fool," I cried, "you loaded it so badly it all fell off."

"No, Massah Donn, dat ain't de way of it. When I was loading up in Hi'kery Holler I'ze smell somefin'."

"Smell what, Shack?"

"Well, Massah Donn, somefin', like brimstone; and I hear a voice, low-down like, say, 'Shack, Shack. Shack,' tree times. Den I got on dat Tom horse and got out ob dat holler mighty quick, I tell ye. Den all of a sudden I hear somefin', as if dat wood was agoin', and I didn't dar look round foh feah de devil take me too."

"Why, Shack, what an old liar you are! What did the devil want with your wood?"

"Why to toast wid, of course. I spec he's mighty nigh out of cord-wood dis winter, and dat ole hi'kery berry good for dat pur- pose."

I am afraid I hastened the demise of this old man by the last trick I played upon him before I was sent away to school. He was the cause of my getting a severe thrashing, and I set about his repayment. While studying up my way to do this I caught a huge tom-cat, that had forsaken the ways of civilized life, in a box-trap set for coons.

Now, it was in midsummer and Shack slept in a little log-cabin built by himself, that had a clapboard roof. I spent nearly a day getting Tom, the cat, into an old boot, head foremost, with noth- ing protuding from the top but Tom's stiff and indignant tail. At night, in the bright light of a harvest moon, armed with a stout cord, and holding to my infuriated prisoner, I softly clam- bered to the roof of Shack's cabin. Cautiously removing the loose clapboards I made a hole immediately above the sleeping body of the Revolutionary body-servant. Looking down I could see the old man sound asleep in the moonlight that streamed through his cabin window. I tied the end of my cord to Tom's tail and let him, yowling, down upon the countenance of my enemy.

Fortunate'y for Shack the infuriated cat struck the head-board instead of the face aimed at. The scratching and yowls awakened Shack, and he arose just as I pulled Tom up for a second and more accurate aim. Shack saw the cat flying, as it were, in mid-air above his head, and with a wild yell of fright he rose up in time to get four claws scratched through his gray wool. He fled through the door towards the house, using every breath he could catch into his lungs in such a yell as never had been heard since the Indians left us. I hastily pulled up my cat, and cutting the cord, saw and heard it go over the roof to the ground with a scratching noise that indicated quite a destruction of clap-boards. Hastily descending, I sought my own bed, from which I came, very like the rest of the family, in wonder at old Shack's disturbance. It would have been taken as a bad dream but for the old negro's scratched and bleeding countenance. As it was, it remained a mystery for years, and Shack to the day of his death told how "de debil come fru de roof," and every time he told the tale he added more horns, bigger eyes, and a larger assortment of tales to the apparition.

Poor old Shack ! his form lies mouldering in the old graveyard, and on the mossy tombstone one can yet read, " *Well done. thou good and faithful servant.* " It is just as well we should think so. Old Shack certainly did.

THE SALES-LADY OF THE CITY.

LILLIAN STUBBS, sales-lady, as she called herself, stood irres-
olute, for a moment, behind the storm-doors of that fashionable
emporium known as Dunn, Dusenborry & Co. It was the hour
for closing, and counters were being draped and lights extin-
guished by the many clerks, preparatory to locking up that
vast establishment for the night.

Well might Lillian Stubbs hesitate making her plunge into
outer night, for it was a cruel cold one, and a furious December
storm was tossing it about. Pulling the hood of her waterproof
closer about her head, and clutching both shawl and light rubber
together in front, so as to shield her thin, naked hands, she bolted
at last into the tumult outside.

It was an awful night. About dark. a qu'et, well-behaved
snow-storm set in, and flakes like feathers fell into the murky
streets. Some roystering winds that were making a night of it far
to the north, hearing of the " beautiful snow," hurried down and
went to ruffling, chasing, and blowing the lovely thing to and fro
in the wildest glee. They did this while shaking shutters, swinging old creaking signs, and knocking venerable chimney-tops into
the street. They drove to shelter all citizens possessed of homes,
while the belated ones, or the unfortunates, were pursued and
buffeted with a fiendish delight that found expression in wild
shrieks ; and up the street and over the house-tops they would
sweep, meeting other winds tearing round corners and whirling into
each other, making lesser storms that sent up in circles snow, soot,
and lighter garbage far into the murky night. The gas lights on
the streets sputtered discouraged, like tallow-dips burned to the
socket.

Through this tempest Lillian Stubbs, sales-lady, struggled

along. At times the winds seemed to seize and hurry her on ; at others, they woul1 smite her in front and make her fairly reel, while pulverized ice mountains appeared to penetrate her thin wraps, until her little white teeth fairly chattered.

Our slender heroine had gained the corner of Elm and Sixth, when she unhappily stepped upon an icy gutter, her feet slipped from under, and she fell with cruel force upon the frozen pavement. For a second she lost consciousness, and when she recovered a strong arm was lifting her from the ground.

" Much hurt, Miss?" asked the kind voice above the strong arm.

" I guess not," she gasped in reply.

The gas above shown clear, in spurts. upon her pale, wet face, and by the same light she saw one half hid in a muffler, surmounted by a silk hat, that seemed nailed to the head, while the overcoat, buttoned to the chin, was of some light-colored cloth. The thought flashed through her mind, half stunned as it was, that her sympathizer was a swell.

"Going far?" again asked the voice.

" Liberty Street," she answered.

" Better take a car."

" If you please."

One of these family carriages of the people at that instant came slowly jingling along. The man hailed it ; and, half carrying his charge. thrust her on the platform into the crowd that thronged the entrance. He elbowed and pushed his way until the girl was well in, and then he paid the conductor for both.

" Get up there, will you?" he said to an old fellow comfortably seated. " This gull has had a tumble, and is hurt." The aged party slowly complied, and the gallant rescuer, after a searching look at his charge, fought his way out, and jumped from the moving car.

The vehicle was densely crowded. Fifty people made a dead weight behind the weary mules, that a brutal driver of a brutal corporation was whaling along. It was hard on the mules, but kind to Lillian, for the crowd made the interior warm to her. Of course the corporation can afford nothing but wet straw to accommodate a public from which it draws its comfortable dividends.

Lillian had four squares to walk, after she left the car, before reaching home. Stiff and sore from her fall, she fairly stumbled into the wretched home, and nearly fainted as she sank into a chair. The house consisted of three rooms. Poverty and sickness drove the family into one apartment. Want was written in dirt over every part of it. It was warmed by fever and an old cook-stove. A dirty, dim coal-oil lamp made privation visible. Two children, gaunt-eyed and ragged, were scraping an old skillet. A half-grown, frowsy girl was turning slapjacks on the stove. The mother, a hard, hook-nosed creature, was doing up a bundle of overalls she had but finished at the sewing-machine. On a low bed in a corner was the father, evidently ill.

"What's up now, Lil?" he asked.

"Got a fall that broke every bone in my body, and then I'm frozen through and through."

"I wish I could give you a liitle of my fever. I am burning up," he growled.

"I had to take a car," the girl continued, "or I'd never got home."

"You did not waste money on a car?" exclaimed the mother.

"No, I didn't, for the swell that helped me up, seeing how poor I was, paid my fare."

"A swell, eh!" cried the father. "He'll be around to get his pay out uv you, an' ef he does, I'll brain him wi'h my hammer—I will."

"Don't worry yourself, dad; I can take care of myself—in a poor way;" and she went to eating, ravenously, the heavy cakes her sister tossed to her, as if she were a dog.

A few days after this, Lillian was at her post near the gorgeous entrance to the fashionable dry-goods store of Dunn, Dusenberry & Co. She went on duty at seven in the morning and left at seven in the evening. She had a rest of half an hour at noon, in which to eat her miserable lunch, and, with this exception, was on her feet through that long stretch; and, when not serving customers, was expected to be busy brushing and rearranging the goods under her charge.

For this labor she received all of three dollars a week. Her mother made overalls at eighty cents a dozen, and her father, when able to work, got a dollar a day.

We spent a great quantity of sympathy—our money and blood —in behalf of the negro slaves at the South, born, through untold generations, to unrequited toil. We cannot see a worse slavery here. The slavery that tortures in our midst has our own s nsitive flesh and blood that are made to suffer. The negro, when well, was fed, clad, and sheltered by the master ; when sick, he was doctored and nursed by his owner ; when he died, the slave-driver buried him. Our slaves feed, c'othe, and shelter themselves; when sick, they nurse and doctor themselves ; when dead, the township buries and the doctors dissect the r bodies.

Old Phineas Dunn, of Dunn, Dusenberry & Co., came into life on a doubt. Nature hesitated whether to work up certain refuse material into a man or a buzzard. The stuff on hand was not good enough for a human being, but was too good for a buzzard. Nature, more from whim than kind impulse, resolved in favor of a man, and Phineas Dunn was set on end, with all the cruel, grasping instincts of a buzzard. Long slender, gaunt, and greedy, he ha a stereotyped smile—a regular mask of a grin—for his customers and a real scowl for his slaves. To the one he was as tyrannical as to the other he was servile and obsequious.

No one had ever seen Dusenberry, no one had ever known the " Co.." and it was a belief among the more knowing that Dusenberry was dead and that old Phineas had frozen out the " Co ," so that the entire firm walked the earth in the form of the venerable but not venerated Dunn.

This hard old miser is not alone in his cruel oppression of helpless women. He makes one of a large class and that class Christian civilization calls for instant suppression. Women are employed as clerks. not because they are efficient and therefore desirable. but for that they are cheap. Women customers hate female clerks. " sales ladies " as they call themselves because the main part of the intense satisfaction found in shopping is in the chaffing that is supposed to lessen prices and effect bargains. The female mind is impressed with the belief that her charms can influence the male specimen on the other side of the counter.

Then, again, whether profits do accrue or not, it is a mild sort of flirtation that even the most sedate cannot resist. This is all utterly rendered null and void with a girl for a clerk. The poetry of life found in shopping is lifted from the business, and with it goes all hopes of bargains. Women instinctively hate each other, and when the fair customer rustles majestically along the centre of the well-stored display of goods she feels as if she were an honest cruiser sailing down a double row of armed enemies of a piratical sort. She knows that she is being gazed on with malicious eyes, her dress mentally criticised, her movements commented on, her pocket-book measured and sneered at. When she tackles one of the enemy, it is with a sneer that destroys all entertainment and banishes all hope of bargains.

Therefore it is that merchants accept female clerks under protest, and engage them only because they are cheap. The competition that is fierce and without reason favors enslavement. For one vacancy there are twenty applicants, and price and labor no consideration, and the poor creatures are abused in a way to fill houses of infamy, hospitals, and graves. A man's tyranny is measured only by his power to abuse. It is not controlled even by his interest. There is something in us— God knows why it should be —that gives a fiendish pleasure in the torture of the dependent, and when to this we add the miserly instincts of trade, we realize the white slavery of helpless women.

We have, in all cities, an army of good women devoted to charitable work. Here is work for them. Let them give the Phineas Dunns to understand that they are in danger of fashionable "boycotting" unless they raise the wages and amend their treatment of these slaves of the yardstick. Of course this will not be done. The e fashionable ladies who go about distributing stoves, coal, and flannels, are animated only by a wish to see their names in print, associated with those of high social position, and known as public benefactors. To do anything so radical and effective as what I suggest, is as wild as if I were to ask them to be kind to, and considerate of, their own servants.

Lillian Stubbs, sales-lady, had one of the most trying and unhealthy positions in the storehouse. Near one of the doors, and almost above a register, she got overheated from the one, and a chill whenever the storm-door opened and let in a column of freezing air. Her feet were frosted from exposure, in her old worn-out shoes, and it was only a question of time as to when she would succumb and be carried to the hospital.

Some days after her fall, she was busy at her post. A little romance had woven itself into spider-like existence, from her shallow brain, over that incident. Who was it who so kindly and tenderly lifted her into the car t at night? It was not Reuben Springer, for he was dead. It could not be Julius Dexter, for he did not wear swell clothes. Nor was it David Swinton ; he deals only with classes. He was, evidently, a young man in gorgeous apparel.

While thus her absurd mind ran on as she dusted and rearranged her goods, she noticed a man standing over the register and regarding her with a puzzled expression, as if in doubt about knowing her. He was a vulgar, over-dressed fellow, of about thirty-five or forty, of slender yet sinewy build. He wore a plum-colored overcoat, lavender kids, patent-leather shoes, and a shiny silk hat. His face was pale, the expression cruel and cunning. He seemed to solve his doubt, for, stepping to the counter, he said, in a soft, low voice to Lillian :

" Glad you got over your fall, miss."

" It wasn't much." she responded, "but I thank you all the same. I b lieve I owe you for my car-fare,"

" No, you don't, I was glad to help you."

Further conversation was prevented by the approach of a woman, who, touching the over-dressed good Samaritan on the arm, said :

"Come on ; I've got what I want, and I'm hungry."

Lillian Stubbs' knowledge of man was defective. She could not distinguish a vulgar fellow from a fashionable swell. But when she hit her own sex she was mo e at home, and in the loud get-up of the painted creature before her she saw a soiled dove that it was her womanly duty to s one to death at all times and on all occasions.

After that it was seldom Lillian walked home of an evening

that she did not have the man her companion. He had informed her that his name was Clarence Fitz James Allen ; that he was the son of a wealthy old duffer who had disowned him because of his refusal to marry a lovely girl said paternal duffer had selected ; and he spun out a dime novel about himself that Lillian accepted as fact, although she felt rather than knew that the fell w was lying. Like the rest of us, she believed that which she wished to believe. Poor girl ! her life was hard, and so hopeless, that this little episode proved too precious to be given up lightly. She felt satisfied that this noble youth loved her ; and it was the first time in her dreary life that love came to lift its hard realities into fairyland.

Clarence Fitz James, etc., was liberal with his money. Every night he took the little shop-girl to a restaurant and ordered a sumptuous repast for both. Clarence Fitz James drank sparingly, and seemed anxious to get the poor girl to indulge. She touched the beer gingerly—really not liking it. But if a fourth of a glass set her tongue to going more liberally than usual the lover seemed delighted. He was, for some reason, deeply interested in the character and ways of old Phineas Dunn. He listened eagerly to the mean and miserly treatment of the clerks. He learned that the old Shylock was too stingy and suspicious to have a watchman on the inside of his store at night, but kept two employed watching the premises from the outside, front and rear. He locked the store-door and the storm-door himself, and put the keys in his own pocket.

One night Clarence Fitz James, etc., treated his love to seats in the orchestra at the Grand Opera House. After the performance, he gave her an oyster supper, and at that supper offered himself as her future husband, and, being accepted, bound the engagement by a large diamond ring, and then made a rather startling proposition. It was that the sales-lady, his *fiancée*, should procure an impression on wax of the key to the storm-door of old Dunn's store. He gave a rather confused and contradictory statement of why he wanted this impression, but said that it was for a gent who would give five hundred dollars for the impression. Clarence produced from his pocket the lump of wax on which the impression was to be made, and as Lillian knew where the key hung during the day, it would be easy to procure what he desired. As soon as he got the five hundred, they should be married, and then he would take his bride to the palace of his noble father and plead forgiveness.

Lillian Stubbs was not altogether idiotic, and she understood precisely what her lover meant. But the girl was in love, and compromised the iniquity by believing that her noble lover was being used by some great burglar who proposed to relieve old Dunn of some of his surplus stock. Her first impulse was to denounce the wicked scheme and say good-by to the man who had proposed it to her. But the beautiful ring glittering on her thin, hard-worked hand, and a glance at the kind, anxious face—the only face that had ever been kind to her—made her hesitate, and in the hesitation she gave way, and, like many of us, compromised by accepting the lump of wax, and saying she would think over it.

That night, or, rather, morning, Lillian found her parents up and awaiting her return.

" Well, you trollop !" cried the paternal Stubbs, " where have you been all this night ? "

" Come, out with it," added the mother, with yet more wrath in her demand.

"I have been to the theatre with Clarence Fitz James Allen, my future husband," boldly responded the girl.

" Fitz hell !" roared the father ; " you have brought your pigs to a pretty market, to be sure. Now, hear me, girl. My brother Tom, you know, is on the force, and he has been here telling us all about it ; how you've been philanderin about with Peg Alick, the well-known house-breaker and thief. What've you got to say fer yourself, you hussy? If I was able I'd take a strap to you."

The poor girl was stunned ; she stammered and wept, and then made a full confession of all that had occurred between her and her proposed husband, not omitting the diamond ring and the offer of $500.

The father received the story in wrathful blasphemy, and avowed his intentions to have the scoundrel jailed immediately. The mother, however, was in deep thought. Five hundred dollars appeared to her a great fortune. So, after the father had exhausted wrath and epithets, she said :

" I don't know about thus. Why not get the thief's five hundred? Let Lil put any key on his wax, get the money, and then turn him over to the p'lice."

"Good enough !" cried the father ; "serve him right. Do it, Lil."

And Lil did as she was bidden. Clarence Fitz James, *alias* Peg Alick, took the wax impression tenderly, but with eagerness, and, in proof of his good faith and generous impulse, thrust a roll of money in the girl's hand. Poor child ! she stood forlorn amid the ruins of her fairy castle, sick and indignant at the deception practised upon her.

The mother's cunning did not end with the capture of Peg's money. Giving her daughter fifty dollars of the treasure, she locked the rest in an old bureau, and said :

" We'll go to old Dunn and tell him how we saved his store, and he's bound to promote you."

To the venerable Shylock of the yardstick they went, and, in an interview in his little private office, the mother told her story. It was comical to note the effect it had upon him. His cold, steely eyes seemed to start from his narrow forehead, while his ash-tinted face fairly mottled in pale splotches, as the revelation revealed the purposed crime. When the key business was reached, he looked up, with a scared expression, and hastily clutching the innocent instrument, he thrust it in his pocket. When the story ended, he gasped for breath, and seemed to be pumping his emotions from some unknown depth.

" Great heavens !" he cried in falsetto spurts, "have we been harboring the associate of burglars? Go away, women ! go away !" And he hurried them through the long store-room to the street, looking anxiously to the right and left, lest they should pilfer some valuables on their way out.

"The nasty old sneak !" exclaimed the mother, when the two were alone ; "just to think of serving us that way, when we saved him thousands ! Never mind, Lil, we have the money, and we'll dress up right smart and get a better place right off."

The girl was delighted with the proposition. She had seen,

day after day, a gorgeous wrap offered in a show-window in Fifth Street, at a very low price, and her female soul longed for its possession. To this place she led her mother. The Hebrew proprietor received them with that insinuating politeness peculiar to such dealers in fashionable raiment.

"Dot berline vas made vur Madame Langdry," he claimed, "pon my shoal it vas. She made dot deposite ven she ordered it, and den she not like it, and ve zells 'em vor notings."

The women, woman-like, tried to reduce this nothing, and at last ended by offering one-half the price at first demanded. With much protestation the dealer accepted, and Lillian counted the money into his eager, and, I must say, rather dirty hands. After receiving the money, which he eyed closely, he proposed giving a receipt, and was gone so long the women began to wonder whether the polite child of Israel could write. He returned at last, accompanied by a policeman, and put the two unfortunates in custody for attempting to pass counterfeit money!

Our police, as a general thing, is a political body, developed by our self-government, and is organized to influence, and, if possible, control the polls, in behalf of the party calling it into existence. This is its main purpose, and during its leisure moments, between elections, it dabbles in arrests for crimes. Now, a criminal may commit any offence, but one, with comparative safety. If the offender is not a very stupid bungler he can always compromise the crime charged by a divide with the sufferer and the police. The one exception, in a list running from murder down to petit larceny, is that which touches our currency. This is a serious business, and the counterfeiter, or his agent in passing false money, is hunted down and punished without mercy.

The mother Stubbs and her poor daughter were hurried to the lockup, and the detectives, searching the hovel, found conclusive proof of guilt in the $450 of miserable counterfeits concealed in the old bureau. But for Uncle Tom, of the force, the two women would have fallen into the hands of a shyster, and found their way to the penitentiary. As it was, Tom saw the Chief of Police, and the two interviewed the Judge of the Criminal Court, and the last named ordered their release, retaining them only as witnesses against

Peg Alick, who had been caught trying to break into the fashionable emporium of Dunn. Dusenbury & Co.

Before the discharge could be effected, Lillian, worn down by hard work, and suffering from shame, excitement, and exposure, was attacked with fever, and carried delirious to the hospital. She awakened from the delirium, but never rallied from the fever. All that science could do, in the hands of skilful Doctor Murphy; all that care in nursing by the good Sisters could contribute, were at the service of the poor slave of the yardstick.

They came too late. She was down with a disease that baffled medicine—that might be called a malignant attack of Dunn, Dusenbury & Co. She, who had sweated under a heat of summer that marked 90° in the shade, and scurried on, with wet feet and frozen body, through the storms of winter, to her twelve hours' daily toil, unnoticed and almost unknown, had, when unavailable, all the care and skill that are given the most fortunate.

Poor little homely wretch ! There was not much of the heroic in her, but it was pitiable to see this great brute of a world sacrificing her miserable life to its selfish greed. Hour after hour, fever wasted her form, and death stamped his seal upon her ashy, pinched face, as, with half-closed eyes, she heard the subdued roar of the great traffic pounding along the stony horror of the bouldered streets, under which she had gone down to death. And, while dying in that warm, but bare and painfully clean ward, how many thousands of her sisters were struggling in the winter's cold for a bare subsistence ; how many thousands, driven on by starvation, were giving their homeless bodies to beastly gratification of men's lust. " Holy Mary. mother of God ! " when will the crucifixion end? From the killing of Our Saviour, we go on, through the ages, torturing, debasing, and destroying those from whose class come our mothers, sisters, and daughters.

The dimmed rays of a wintry sun shone through a curtainless window, in its setting, upon the still couch that a good sister approached softly, in prayer, to close the glazed eyes and fold meekly upon the sunken breast the thin hands of the Dead Slave. Upon one finger yet shone the Mock Diamoi d, that gleamed like a mock light from our decayed, Christian civilization.

MONTEZUMA HAWKINS, REFORMER.

MONTEZUMA HAWKINS, Friend of Man, sat at his noon-day meal. The room in which this banquet was held indicated extreme economy or privation in its occupant. The ceiling was low, and not much of it. It started some seven feet from the floor, ran parallel for half the width of the room, and then seemed to get discouraged and fell away rapidly until but two feet made its supporting wall at the other end. One window on that side, of small dimensions, let in the light to exhibit the furniture that was neither choice, rare, nor antique. A cot, thrust into one corner, met the descend ng ceiling on one side, and held a mattress of straw that once, in its early youth, seemed stuffed with grasshoppers, but had evidently given up its young elasticity, and was as hard as the heart of an alderman. The bed-clothes indicated former circumstances of cleanliness, while the pillow was of that diminutive sort that looked as if the sleeper had to hold on with both hands to keep it from slipping up his nose or disappearing in an ear. A pine table and three chairs, if not strangers to each other, of that various make that indicated second-hand auction-rooms, when the drift of poverty gathers in a great city.

Montezuma Hawkins' banquet was in keeping with his surroundings, and consisted of a section of bologna sausage—that compound of red flannel, pepper, and pork—a sandwich, so called, because of the thin slice of dyspepsia held between two heavy layers of in igestion, and water nicely warmed by the summer air in a brown stone pitcher.

The proprietor of this apartment, and the consumer of this banquet, ate rapidly, and as he did so, he quite as eagerly turned over the leaves and read from a book that he held in his left hand, while he helped himself to food with his right.

No artist would select Montezuma Hawkins as a model for an Apollo. He appeared to be about twenty-eight or thirty years of age, and he ran to length, without the proportionate breadth and thickness. His front and rear elevations, as an architect would say, suggested the Washington monument. His legs were long and slender ; his body was long and flat ; his face long and sallow. His black hair fell in straight locks from his high, narrow head. His features were in keeping, the more pronounced of them being a nose not prominent, but of unusual length, with a slight elevation at the end, indicative of an inquiring mind. The eyes were prominent, dark, and rather handsome, while his mouth and chin exhibited more sensitiveness than strength. In his movements, that were restless, eager, and anxious, Montezuma Hawkins, Friend of Man, struck a close observer as the embodiment of a fever set on end and endowed with great activity.

Finishing his repast with a drop from the brown pitcher, he took from his pocket a brierwood pipe, filled it with tobacco from another pocket, and, giving a hasty glance at the sunlight creeping in at the one window, he continued his eager reading of the book. In this he was interrupted by a heavy knock upon the door, and, before he could say " Come in," it was thrown open with a bang, and three men entered. They were men of red faces and rough clothes. Montezuma exhibited no surprise at this unexpected intrusion. He nodded familiarly to them, and they nodded in return. Two possessed themselves of the rickety chairs, while the third seated himself upon the table.

" What's up ? " asked the host, continuing to smoke and looking up reluctantly from his book.

" Notice to 'tend a meetin' of delegations at the Brown Jug tonight, to consider what's got to be done in the comin' elections," was the reply from the man on the table.

" That means chin music and beer. Won't go."

" Now look here, Monty," said the man ; " you set up to be a reformer, and you don't reform worth a cent. When we buckle down to the collar, you're in the britchin' ; when we're in the britchin', you're strainin' at the collar. What's the good of that ? "

"I give it up," replied Hawkins; "I am tired of it. No two of you agree on anything but beer and talk. There's no good, Jim Brice, in that. I don't want beer, and I'm too busy for idle talk."

"There's goin' to be something done this time," continued Brice, "and don't you forget it. But you will, and be sorry for it ef you don't come."

"I'll think about it. Now I must go. Time's up, fellows; good day ;" and so the visitors and the visited walked out together. Descending the three flights of steep stairs, and gaining the street, Jim Brice said :

"Take a nip, Monty?"

"Never nip, Jim." And he strode away as the three turned in at the nearest lager-beer saloon.

The three men were political agitators and lived mainly on the agitation. Professing to represent the labor movements, they really made three of a large army who had no more to do with the sons of toil than they had with the Apostles. Hawkins had a contempt for them he did not even care to conceal. It was, therefore, through accident that he attended the meeting.

The casualty came about in this way :

There was a girl, daughter of a widow, in straitened circumstances, very lovely and quite accomplished, who had won the heart of our hero. Clara Callan had bloomed into womanhood, amid commonplace and base surroundings ; but her beauty was not as much above the humble life to which she had been born as were her educational attainments. An only child, the poor widow had starved over scanty food and shivered under scant apparel, to keep her daughter well clad, and at school. The little girl responded admirably to the demand, and became and continued the envy of her classmates at the free school, and the pride of her teachers.

This had come to an end, and the poor girl found herself graduated into a position not provided for, to be either comfortable or pleasant. Too well educated and refined for a servant, she was without the means to live as a lady ; and, looking down upon the associates poverty furnished, she was shut out from the more fortunate who could wait in idleness for the husbands to support them.

While in this state of discontent, she made the acquaintance of Montezuma Hawkins. The son of a drunken bookbinder, the boy had been brought up to the same work, and seemed born to be as sober and industrious as his unfortunate father had been idle and dissipated. At the time I introduce him, he was the sole support of a widowed mother and two maiden sisters, older than himself. Through these sisters he came to know Clara, and was soon her devoted lover. An enthusiast and hard student, the bookbinder gave her some intellectual life, and was a relief to the dull commonplace of her pinched and dreary existence.

The young man's dreams of labor reform and the future elevation of his class through his own exertions, were not only stimulated by his passion, but his hard, rough nature was softened by his love. Dogmatic, impatient, and irritable as he was with his fellow-laborers, he was strangely kind and modest in the presence of this, to him, angel, whose beautiful nature was to be the sunlight of his life.

On the evening I speak of, he had dressed with the usual care for such visits, and went to call upon her. She was not at home, and from lack of aught else to do he dropped in at the Brown Jug. To his surprise, he found the place crowded not only by the rough element common to such places, but on all sides by brother workmen from different associations of organized labor. He soon learned that the matter under consideration was the nomination of an independent ticket for the approaching election.

This project of making labor felt at the polls had been long a favorite with our hero ; but every effort, in which he was aided by a few earnest radicals, had proved a failure, and every year he saw with disgust his fellow-workmen fighting on one side or the other of contests that had in reality nothing at issue of interest to his class. He gave up at last in despair.

The fact is, Montezuma Hawkins, like every other self-made man, had many disagreeable qualities that he took no pains to conceal. His intense egotism, when opposed, found expression in biting sarcasm ; and if pressed further than his short allowance of patience, he would fiercely ride down, as it were, his opponent. Nothing but his purity of character, deep earnestness, and, above all, his power to think aloud on his legs—that his crowd sneered at as "gab" and yet admired—made him tolerated at all. He was greeted from all sides as "Monty," but seldom invited to join any one at the bar, and seemed, as he was, indeed, something separate and apart from the crowd. The men who called him "Monty" to his face, styled him "hog" after he passed. Hawkins, in fact, reciprocated the feeling. He had no confidence in the crowd about him, and soon withdrew, seeking his solitary den to read, far into the night, Henry George's fascinating book on land reform. "Progress and Poverty."

While the noisy, half-intoxicated crew were discussing the proposed movement at the Brown Jug, quite another sort of an assembly had the same subject before it in a room at a fashionable hotel. Instead of rough workmen, or representatives of the bummer element, this collection was composed of the so-called "gentlemen," whose clothes and conduct indicated that they owned something beside themselves, and were easy in their ownership.

"I tell you," said a man of some sixty years, whose bald head shone in the gaslight like a billiard ball, "the Democrats are cutting into us like the devil with the Prohibitionists, and unless we can counter in a labor movement, we may as well hang up the fiddle and the bow."

"I know that," responded a younger man, "and we've been trying to start it, but it won't start."

"These paper-caps have been fooled so often," remarked another, "that they are suspicious and indifferent. They won't listen any longer to the old spavined hacks we have been using."

"Can't we find a new leader?" asked the first speaker.

"I know of one," said a tall, thin-visaged man, "if we could only bag him. He is quite young, lives in a garret on bread and water, and wears clothes scarcely decent, certainly not comfortable, that he may support an old mother and two sisters."

"Such a fellow is no good," chimed in one.

"I don't know about that," said the thin man. "I happened to hear him one night at a free library meeting we got up for workingmen. He has the most wonderful voice and remarkable flow of words I ever listened to. But how to capture him is the question."

" Money?" suggested one.

" Won't work. It would be dangerous to try it. He's just the sort of a crank to howl over the attempt on his virtue. Yet every man has his price. I have been thinking of this and studying the fellow. I think I see the way to his capture."

"What is it? "

" There is a devilish pretty girl who, with her mother, lives in a tenement-house of mine. He is sweet on that girl."

"Don't see it," said the bald-headed man, helping himself to a glass of wine.

"That's a pity," dry'y remarked the cadaverous plotter; "but I believe I do. Harry McLain, are you willing to put yourself at the head of the labor movement?"

"I?" responded the handsome young man thus addressed. " What do you mean?"

" Come out as an independent for Congress on the noble workingman's ticket. Your late affiliation with the Democracy will make it consist."

" Go whooping around with a lot of greasy mechanics? No, I thank you."

"'The main run of voters are greasy, my boy, let them be Republican or Democratic. They are all alike in that respect, as they are all alike when it comes to what they call principles. We furnish the money, the greasy fellows the votes. It won't do to be nice."

"Don't take it," said the young man. ' I don't know anything about their rot. I shouldn't be able to utter a sentence of it."

"It is easier picked up than our rot, my boy. You'll get interested in it when you come to consider the subject. You may think it strange, but all the brain of the country is enlisted on that side. If the fellows had a press, an organization, and some money, they would move our bowels, I can tell you."

A lengthy discussion followed, that held these politicians together far past midnight. It was determined, at last, that young McLain should be put forward as the independent candidate, and his thin, Cassius-like companion undertook his guidance.

Harry McLain was "human, handsome, and liable to debt." His principal business in life seemed to be immediate dissipation of the fortune his overworked father had left him. He had dabbled in politics, for the sake of the excitement, and after a trial of the Democracy turned over to the Republicans, incurring thereby a character for inconsistency that no serious people will tolerate. One may change his opinions frequently as he will, he may avow any, or live upon none, provided he votes the ticket of his party. To vote the ticket is like paying church dues. It is the sanctification of faith and good works.

Not long after the independent movement had been determined on, Montezuma Hawkins and his betrothed were walking in the park. It was the one source of enjoyment they could afford It was something more than enjoyment to the young man. He was deeply in love with his Clara, and every moment in her society was an hour of heaven. Along the dreary pathway of life the softened sunlight fell through the roseate atmosphere, and flowers bloomed and sweet birds sang, as flowers and birds never bloomed nor sang before. It was a strange thing to see this elongated piece of animated egotism, this embodiment of sarcasm and ill-temper, this fierce reformer gazing at this girl, with all the wistful humility of a dog, living on her slightest word and eager to obey her slightest wish.

It was more than strange, it was pitiable, when we know that, with all his awkward ways and disagreeable self-assertion, he had a delicate brain in his head, and a deep, earnest, sensitive heart in his bosom. Of neither did the little girl have the slightest knowledge, or indeed care.

On the day to which I refer, Monty had been promoted to foreman in his shop, and, with the increased wages, he thought he might venture to marry, provided his bride consented to share the house with his mother and sisters.

"That is all very good of you, Monty, dear," she said, when the plan was first proposed; "but what will become of my poor mother?"

Monty knew that the poor mother. so lovingly referred to, had been running a sewing-machine for many years. so that her daughter could be kept at school ; and he knew that to take the daughter off her hands would be a relief.   To undertake the support of the mother would be to leave his own out in the cold.

" We can get rooms of our own, Clara, if you say so." he pleaded; " but then they will not be so well furnished, for I must continue my support of mother and the girls."

" Oh, Monty, do be more patient ! " she cried.   " We must wait a while longer; something will turn up one of these days. We won't always be so poor."

The young man shook his head and sighed.   He felt that his ardent advances had been coldly received. and that his good fortune. found in the promotion. was treated with indifference.

" Monty dear," she said, after a long silence, " why don't you make more speeches ? "

" Speeches ? "

" Yes I said that.   You make beautiful speeches.   I am so proud of you, standing up making the crowd cheer and applaud. I do wish you would."

The unexpected interest shown in him by this angel of light and grace sent a thrill through him that made him gasp almost. Poor fellow! he did not know that it was the whisper of the devil, sent through his love.   He was delighted, yet he responded, after a pause: " I'd like to please you, Clara, but there's nothing in it. I am beset every day by fellows urging me to take the stump for the Independents."

" Oh, do, Monty !   I wish you would; I wish you would, for me."

This was an unexpected interest in a subject never before indulged in, and Monty, looking at her surprised, asked what on earth had given her such a liking for politics.

" Oh, I don't know ! " she replied.   " Yes, I do.   A friend told me that if you'd come out, it would be a great success."

" What friend is so complimentary of my poor powers?" he asked.

She colored, stammered, and then said that it was her mother.

"No," she added, "it was not mother. It makes no odds who it was. I want you to make the speeches."

"I will, if you wish," he replied.

She actually kissed him for his compliance, and the kiss sealed the compact. That night he reported at the headquarters of the Independents, and was almost immediately launched in the canvass,

The display of vitality exhibited by the noble workingmen in this contest was unparalleled. The headquarters were thronged, the night air poisoned by torchlights of processions. Brass bands stunned the ears, while at stands erected in the open air meetings were held, to which came the torchlight processions, and from which, night after night, the Hon. Harry McLain and Montezuma Hawkins, workman, as he was styled, held forth, on the wrongs of the toiling millions. Of the two orators, our friend Monty was far the more popular. As a mere declaimer, he was the best I ever hear. His clear, sweet voice was equalled by his happy facility of expression, in which the choicest words seemed to fit in and flow out on the sentences, as if a great composer had inspired a great piece of music. The crowds responded with cheers to his impassioned appeals. And, really, to those who knew him personally, it was remarkable how he changed in appearance when under the spell of his own inspiratio. His sallow face flushed, his dark eyes gleame, while his gesticulations were not only appropriate but graceful.

He was soon carried along by the excitement he aided in creating, and what began in a wish to gratify the girl he loved, soon passed to an earnest and intense belief in his effort. He first neglected, and then quite abandone, his workshop, for the proprietor happened to be a Democrat, and was quick to resent a movement calculated to defeat his party. During the day Hawkins was busy preparing and mailing documents; at night he was either on the stand addressing crowds in the open air, or visiting lodges and unions, where he urged all his fellow-laborers to take part in the good cause.

The labor movement represented, of course, only one fourth of the conflict going on. Three other parties were as busily at work, and had our oratorical friend been less carried away by his zeal, and given closer attention to what other cool lookers-on saw, he might have found a difficulty in separating the torchlight pro-cessions of the Democrats from their own ; and a Prohibitionist would as well have seen in amazement the Democrats and Tem-perance men so mixed at the meetings as not to be distinguished. One fact Hawkins did observe and puzzle over—that was the lib-eral expenditure of money. Some one, or ones were paying for the long processions, fireworks, and free bars of lager-beer saloons. Hawkins got no solution to the mystery, nor did he make much effort in that direction. Our Roman virtue softens in the light of our own desires. If the enemy was furnishing means to further their own destruction, Heaven forbid that they should be even discouraged, let alone exposed.

Hawkins' fame as an orator spread, and men and women who cared nothing for the cause gathered about the stand to hear the silver-tongued advocate. It was common for the Hon. Harry Mc-Lain to open with a neat speech, made up mainly of solemn com-monplace. Afterward, Montezuma would address the crowd for an hour or an hour and a half. The audience never seemed to weary of his declamation, that was lit by flashes of sarcasm that brought out hearty responses of laughter and cheers.

The orator knew that Clara was among the listeners, and the knowledge inspired him. After a time he missed her sweet, upturned face, and he came to notice that his honorable associate also disappeared from the platform and was seen no more that night. He did not, however, connect the two facts.

Election day came and the vote was heavy ; it almost equalled that of a Presidential contest. That night, Montezuma observed. much to his surprise, that while the Democratic and Republican headquarters were crowded with eager, noisy people, his own were almost deserted. A few stupid cranks alone hung about the tables, and got no returns. The fact was, that the Prohibition rendezvous was in about the same condition. Finding that he could get no returns at either place, he hurried to the Republican headquarters. They were coming in freely, and full statements were given of Democratic and Republican votes, but few or none of the Independent ticket. While wondering at this, he encountered his own boss of the bookbindery where he was employed.

"Well, Monty," he said, wrathfully, "I 'spose you made enough to do without work, laboring for those thieves. Anyway, I don't want you any more."

"What do you mean?" demanded Hawkins.

"Oh! don't play innocence, damn you; it won't go down," and the man turned his back upon him.

Montezuma soon had confirmation of the fact asserted. He was congratulated on all sides by half-drunken politicians for his success in fooling the Democracy. He awakened to the dismal fact that he had been sold by the very class he had sought to destroy. The choicest efforts of his brain, the noblest impulses of his heart, had baited a vulgar trap, and he had been the ridiculous victim of a miserable cheat—that all saw but the victim.

Weary of body and sick at heart, the poor fellow wended his way along the fashionable street to his humble garret. Feeling his humiliation and shame, he fairly shrunk into the shadows of the lofty houses all aglare with light. All was lost to him but one sweet hope, that in this dark hour seemed his resurrection and his life. Above the dark cloud of adversity shone, like a star in a space of blue heaven, the face of Clara. his love. After all, what was the worth of these shadows with such a consolation?

At the moment this thought shot through his frame and lifted his manhood into his better self-respect, while he was saying to himself, "In all this world I have but one who believes in and loves me, but that one is an angel worth them all," he happened to look up and into a plate-glass window of a fashionable restaurant. He started as if a wave of electricity had been shot into him. At a little table, laughing and eating, he saw two people. One was unmistakably his friend and brother-orator, Harry McLain, but the other——. A mist came upon the poor fellow's eyes, and, amid the falling sleet—for winter had suddenly come upon the town—he staggered against a lamp-post and stared as if distraught. It was the face of *Clara*—his Clara. his love! But, oh, how changed! Rich feathers fell over her lovely face, costly jewelry adorned the white column of her neck, a rich dress partly exposed the snowy precipice of her dazzling shoulders; and she gazed with those soft, dreamy eyes on this man as she had never looked upon the poor bookbinder. Great God! what a revelation and revolution!

How poor Montezuma got to his garret he could not have told himself. He did get there. Lighting his lamp with mechanical impulse and precision, he set it upon the table, and, taking a key from his pocket, unlocked and opened an old box. From this he took a package of notes and letters. Well worn they were, those oft-read missives. Then he picked out some little womanly presents—poor in material, but delicately wrought by female fingers, that seemed to weave in the threads the tenderest affections of the worker. For nearly an hour he sat with these things in his trembling hands, and gazed upon them with a dead, stony expression that was pitiable. He was too strong to weep, too weak to kill. His neck was slender, and the base of his skull was not rounded out with those animal passions that make the man feared. And so, between the two, he suffered an agony that would have made that of the cross itself a lesser punishment.

Rising wearily at last, he left his room without extinguishing the lamp, and strode on through the night and the storm to the house occupied by Clara. Ascending two flights of stairs, he paused upon the landing, and shrunk into one corner, where, crouching down, he could remain concealed. He knew instinctively that Clara had been taken to some place of amusement, and shuddered with horror, not with cold, at the thought of how much longer than the play would take he would have to wait her return.

Hour after hour went slowly by. He heard the noises of the street die out, and ever and anon some people, in groups or singly, would come up the steps and pass him. Once a female garment swept across his knees, and he heard doors open and shut as the lodgers of the building sought their rooms. At last, away past midnight, he heard wheels rattle up and stop at the entrance below. There was a gleam of light, his quick ear caught the low uttered "Good-night," and then the light, well-remembered step upon the stairs.

It was Clara. She paused on the landing, without seeing him of course, and opened the door with a night-latch, that she handled so delicately that she had entered before he was aware. Fortunately she left the door ajar, and he noiselessly followed. She, dexterously striking a match, lit a lamp, and the haggard, love-stricken man stood before her. Her clamped teeth caught the scream her heart sent up, and she seized a chair-back to keep from falling.

"Oh, Monty!" she exclaimed, in an undertone, "how you frightened me!"

"Clara!" he said. His low, sweet voice seemed to thrill through her, as he touched the rich sealskin sacque that had partly fallen from her shoulder. "I don't ask where you got this livery of hell. I have only to say that, in getting it, you walk over the body of the one honest man who loves you better than life."

The girl's face flushed and then paled, showing out in painful contrast the rouge upon her cheeks. Then she wailed piteously, as the tears started from her eyes:

"Monty, Monty! don't be hard on me. I could not help it."

"Oh, no," he responded bitterly; "you would rather be a rich man's mistress than a poor man's wife."

"Don't be hard on me! don't be hard on me! I pity you, Monty—and, oh! God, I pity myself. But, Monty, I would have been only a burden to you."

And the tears streamed from her eyes.

"Clara," he said, taking her hand, "come to me yet—come now. I love you, Clara. I never knew till this hour how much I love you. Now don't—don't say anything. Wait, think—you hold my life in your little hands. That man don't love you. We will forget him." And no dumb creature begging for its life ever put in an eager face such a piteous expression of appeal.

I am sorry to write of the miserable condition of my po r hero. I am pained to add that his crawling humility was met, on the part of the girl, with a feeling of disgust and aversion. Had he gone out and killed the betrayer; had he even flung her tokens and gifts in her face, as he had intended, he would have stood a better chance for the wicked and ruined love he solicited. Clara crowded down her disgust, and, woman-like, threw a grace over her refusal.

"Monty," she said, "I love you too well to listen. I can degrade myself; I cannot degrade my husband—for that is what you mean. Monty, let us submit. We are, as you have said night after night, the slaves—you to your unrequited toil; I to my shame. They own us, Monty; they own us."

I cannot dwell on this scene. He begged, poor fellow, on his knees, and the more he grovelled and debased himself, the firmer she grew. Poets have sung of the generous, self-sacrificing quality of love. It is a lie. There is no more cruel, selfish, and implacable passion given humanity. Love of the handsome Harry McLain made Clara a beast, and sent her old lover down to death, and she knew it.

Let me make a finish of the little left. Two days after this parting the horror stricken mother and sisters of poor Monty found his body in a kneeling position in his garret, one end of his suspenders around his neck and the other tied to a hook in the wall. The sisters saw through their tears, in the suspenders that served as a rope, a gift worked by the fair fingers of Clara Callan.

THE WHARF-RAT.

NOVEL XI.

ONCE upon a time a slender little street Arab, without parents and of course without a home, who sold papers in the morning and polished shoes in the afternoon, found on an abandoned piece of a raft an old barrel that he converted into a bedroom. By shifting the open end of his apartment to the leeward of cold nights, and covering himself well with shavings and straw, the poor boy slept the sleep of peace and innocence. The rain pattering upon his barrel and the dashing waves of the great river only lulled his slumbers to a deeper rest ; and, although he did not thank God for his shelter—for the waif was untaught—he had about the same sense of thanksgiving that a bird or houseless dog might have on finding a safe retreat from harm.

The river on which the lad rested had extremes of high and low water. In midsummer his old wreck was high and dry on a sandbar ; in spring and autumn it rode upon the waves. One morning, in an unusual flood, the old rotting structure broke away, and, with its sleeping occupant, swept out into the stream. That part of the little fellow, common to all of us, that never sleeps, wakened him, and at first he was somewhat startled to find himself and his home on the highway to New Orleans.

He was however a born wharf-rat, and knew that he could plunge in and swim ashore, let the shore be ever so far ; but he mourned the loss of his home. Like a self-reliant, plucky little chap as he was, he determined to cling to his possessions to the last moment of hope ; and, so resolving, he sat down and gazed about him.

He gazed as well as he could, for it was yet night. The long, heavy rain-storm had passed. The stars were bright, shining through the purified atmosphere ; and from either bank the high chimneys of manufactories vomited red flames that shone in paths on the river, dazzling the eyes in places, and leaving all else in a deeper gloom. The lad sat and shivered in the cold, wondering much what next would happen.

He was not left long in doubt. Suddenly a huge mass, with gleaming open furnaces and a roar like distant thunder, bore toward him. It was a steamboat, and was coming so directly upon him that the lad made ready to plunge and swim for his life ; but while, with a coolness his career of self reliance had taught him, he hesitated, in order to select the side for his swim, so as to avoid the wheel, he realized somehow that the steamer was rounding to for a landing. This saved the little raft, and, although it was tossed wildly in the wake of the steamboat, the lad clung to his old home.

While doing so, and almost under the towering side of the steam-er, he heard something fall, splashing, into the water. This might be a stick of wood or a bucket of slops that disturbed the waves, and the lad settled himself to looking again at this dark uncertainty in the face. The waves of the steamer had floated his frail struct-ure out into the stream, and our little hero became aware of the fact that he was making one of a string of strange articles being carried along by the flood. In the deepening gloom, for he had passed the furnaces that lined the bank, he could not make out his neighbors, other than dark objects half submerged, some of which grated and sawed against one another, as if quarrelling in the contact, while others moved on in silence.

The roseate streaks of day dawned along the east, and soon apace the sun came up in clouds, for the bright, clear night dis p-peared in a haze, and day's huge luminary seemed a larger moon, so shorn was it of light. The scene about our little hero was not en-couraging ; a vast yellow flood of water, spread above the river's banks, opened on each side. Immediately about him a long streach of floating trees, boxes, barrels, stumps, outhouses, and pens swept along with him, while a steamboat, breasting the current, and therefore keeping from the centre, came roaring along.

At the sight of this source of rescue, the lad did not cry out or wave any signal of distress. Young as his life was, he had learned the bitter lesson taught us all, and that was that to stop a huge steamboat to rescue one little life would be an absurdity quite outside all Christian calculations of charity. I put the case too strongly. The fact is, Rat Ely, as he was known among his brother newsboys, did not consider that he was in any peril, only somewhat puzzled by the abrupt change being made in his surroundings. He therefore drew from his barrel the provisions he had put aside the night before for his breakfast; and, with sharp little teeth, went to eating the chunk of bread and slices of ham a kind hearted woman had given him.

While thus engaged he happened to glance along a tree, the trunk of which touched his raft as the two floated along; and he saw resting on a limb ahead of him the body of a man. Rat dropped his breakfast, and, seizing the bark of the trunk with his muscular little hands, he pulled along until he brought himself within reach of the body. Resting for a few moments, he then seized upon the coat of the man; and, with infinite labor and after a long time, succeeded in rolling the body in on his raft.

Rat saw that his find was handsomely dressed. Indeed, the glitter of a heavy gold chain on the vest made the lad's eyes fairly gleam. He was about to seize it, when the dead glare of the half-opened eyes made him shudder and draw back. He turned from the body, looked over the waters, and then went to gnawing at his bread again. The lad knew that at the end of that chain there was a watch. He reasoned that a man possessed of a watch must have a pocketbook, and he thought how cunning it would be to possess himself of the valuables and then tumble the body back into the water.

The boy had about determined on this, when, looking again at his treasure, he saw a cut on the man's head, which was bleeding afresh. While he gazed the man moved. Rat's eyes opened in amazement, and he continued to stare at the sufferer until the man, after a brief struggle, sat up. The unfortunate gazed in a dazed way at the lad for some time, and then asked in a voice scarcely above a whisper, how he got where he found himself.

" Fished ye out," responded the boy, with a nod at the river.

The man, drawing his feet from the water slowly and with

difficulty, as if very weak, sat pondering, with the blood dripping
from his head, as if vainly endeavoring to pull his mind together.
At last he pointed to the breast-pocket of his overcoat, and said
in a whisper : " Get it out." Thus instructed, the lad thrust in
his hand, and produced a leather-covered flask. Unscrewing the
stopper, he put the flask to the man's mouth, and the poor fellow
drank eagerly of the contents. This seemed to revive him, but
brought on a chill that shook him from head to foot. Again and
again he drank, and then offered it to his preserver. Rat Ely took
one swallow of the fiery liquor, and then, nearly choking, handed
the flask hastily back. The man smiled faintly, and then, much
strengthened, said :

" Well, my, lad, what can we do now ? "

Rat pointed to a couple of men in a skiff not far off. One of
the men was pulling at the oars, while the other, standing in the
boat, was gazing at the drift as if in search of something more
valuable than logs. The sufferer on the raft threw up his hand,
and the boat was headed toward them. As it drew near, the back
of the man rowing was toward them, but the face of the fellow
standing came in full view. Rat's companion hastily thrust his hand
into his bosom, and drawing out a Russia leather book, long and
flat, handed it to the boy, telling him in an undertone to hide it.
Rat thrust it under the shavings of his bed in the barrel. The
bow of the skiff was thrust in over the raft, and the man, standing
erect, asked, with an oath, how the two got there.

" That's not the question," answered the rescued, with apparent nonchalance ; " what we are considering is how to get
out. See here, men, I will give you all my money (some $80) and
a reward besides, to get us safely ashore."

The men in the skiff conversed in an undertone with each other
for a moment, and then the spokesman of the two seized the
rescued and pulled him into the skiff. Rat Ely turned to secure
the hidden book, when the skiff was shoved off, leaving him on
the raft. He heard his friend remonstrating as he seized the arm
of the man who had pulled him in, and saw him pushed down,
and the boat rowed rapidly away toward the shore.

Rat Ely felt angry, of course, but he was so accustomed to

rough treatment in his young life that his indignation was short-
lived, and he gazed after the skiff and its occupants until they
were lost in the hazy distance. Then he turned his attention to
his own unpleasant condition. After a time, he drew the book
from the barrel, and, opening it, found a mass of water-soaked
papers. The boy could not read print, although a newsboy, let
alone writing, but he tenderly unfolded the sheets and spread
them out to dry. As the sun rose brighter in the heavens, the
mist lifted and disappeared, giving way for the warm rays to assist
in the task. The papers soon lost their dampness; but the leather
case remained so wet for hours that he could not replace the
documents This, however, was at last accomplished, and the
boy, lost in replacing the papers, did not notice a boat that, approaching, gave out a hearty hail. Looking out, he saw a large
ferryboat, worked by horses, laden with people.

"What ar' ye doin' thar?" cried the man in command.

"Nuthin," responded the boy.

"Well, hurry through and git aboard."

Rat, thrusting the package in his bosom, and picking up the
flask that had been dropped on the raft, responded, and scram-
bled up over the side of the boat, nimble as a squirrel. No further
attention was paid him by the master of the raft. A stout woman
with a kind face tried to draw out of the boy some account of his
adventures, but, meeting with no encouragement, abandoned the
attempt. Rat watched his home float off, but took the loss with
the sense of the inevitable to which he had been trained. With
the same quiet indifference, he accepted his rescue. The flood
had submerged the village bluff where they landed, and while the
passengers, horses, and wagons disappeared in the town, Rat remained upon the wharf-boat, with his box and brushes strung
over his shoulder, well knowing that, sooner or later, a steamboat
would come puffing along, on which he proposed returning to the
city. This happened in an hour after his landing; and, waiting
his opportunity as the steamboat was moving out, he sprang aboard
and disappeared among the pile of boxes and barrels like a veri-
table rat.

Our little hero returned to the city and plunged again into his fierce fight for existence. He had suffered a severe loss in the great calamity of a flood such as the country had never seen before. His house was gone, and had he been called upon to make an assignment the remaining assets would not have paid a cent on the dollar ; but, as he had no creditors, that formality was not pressed upon him. Had he taken account of stock, which he did not, he would have found himself possessed of his health, brushes, blacking-box, and the indomitable energy of Armand Richelieu sung of by the lascivious Bulwer. Rat Ely did not read the papers he dealt in. Certain striking features of the sensational daily sewers he dealt out were given him and his comrades, and these at that time were, "All About the Flood," and a particularly interesting execution of a brutal murderer that the cultured wives and children of the reading public were permitted to enjoy.

Had the Rat read his wares, he would have found that he had taken part in a mystery which was then agitating the social world, and which told of the strange disappearance of a prominent citizen.

Mr. Arnold Stevens had left Central Pennsylvania, where he had converted an inheritance from an uncle into bonds to the amount of fifty thousand dollars, and, returning home, had diverged to a point in Virginia where he had relations and some business. From this point he had travelled to the village of Clamdon on the river, where he took the steamboat *Helen Marr* for home. As the boat was expected to land at the city in the night, Mr. Stevens did not retire to his stateroom, but spent the time at cards with three passengers in the cabin. When informed that the steamboat was about to round-to for the wharf, he went to his stateroom to put on his overcoat and secure his satchel. This was the last seen of him. As the stateroom opened upon the guard, by another door, that would be nearer the city, the boat clerk supposed he had gone out that way and so got ashore. The three passengers who had been playing cards with him also disappeared.

Some days after, a lumberman getting a load of boards from a yard found Mr. Stevens' satchel cut open and the contents scattered about the place.

Here was a clue to foul play that the police seized on. From it. policeman-like, they worked up a theory, in which they were aided by Mr. Stevens' creditors, to the effect that the unfortunate man had made off with his fifty thousand dollars, and had, while doing so, cut open his own valise as a blind. It was soon found that a disreputable woman had disappeared at the same time, and, although Mr. Stevens left a wife and family, to whom he was tenderly attached, in the deepest grief and financial distress, nothing could shake the efficient police in their cunning theory and cruel result.

The one little brain that could have solved the mystery was not called on nor consulted.

In his ten years of life the Rat had grown cunning and cautious. He had but one hope, and that was his daily subsistence, and but one fear, and that was the police. Once in his life a drunken Kentuckian had given him a valuable pin. In attempting to realize on this. he had been seized and sent to what we are pleased to call a " Reform School " for six months. The little Arab had not only pined in his prison, but got so much " reform," bad food, and a stick that he wisely resolved never to have any " reform in his " again.

The hair-mattressed and linen-sheeted world that grumbles in its morning rest at the newsboys' cries at daylight, little dream of the privations from which these ragged Mercuries emerge, yelling, as they run along. the " news," which the Hoe presses have been throwing off at the dead hour of the night. From arched ways and areas, from damp cellars and suffocating tenement rooms, half clad and all starved, these homœopathic doses of humanity swarm out with a fierce activity that tells what they may come to be if they grow to manhood. It is fortunate for " society " that only the more rugged and tough survive, for there is here the raw material being worked up to feed jails and fill penitentiaries, with, at intervals, the skull of a born murderer to supply the gallows.

Among these Rat Ely found place. His first sleeping apartment was in the area of a restaurant. where the hot steam made warm the half-dozen boys huddled together, but had the exasperating—indeed, at times, maddening—odor of cooking, that brought to their empty stomachs a realizing sense of their keen demands. As winter melted in the warmth of spring, the little fellow, with a partner, found an old store box in the back yard of a shop, that they fitted up with shavings and bits of old carpet, so that it served their purpose for the half-nights they gave to sleep.

Rat Ely's wearing apparel was more comfortable than elegant. It consisted mainly of a woollen jacket, a world too wide for his slender body, and which, reaching to his knees, concealed his lack of underwear. In the huge breast-pocket of this he concealed his treasures, together with such scraps of food as, dog like, he could gather from waste barrels set out to be carted off by dealers in such refuse. Of the two treasures, Ely's affections centred on the silver-mounted flask that he often contemplated with the delight of a miser, and from which he, from time to time, tasted sparingly, quite pleased with the cheerful frame of mind that followed. He, however, regarded with some awe the book his unfortunate friend so earnestly sought to hide. Poor boy, he little dreamed that he was carrying hid in his bosom a wealth for which many a man, high in the social scale, would barter his soul. So little did he know of this that often, when suffering from the pangs of hunger, he was tempted to offer it for a mince pie or a slice of cake. He was wild for sweets, the quality of a healthy stomach, as the tastes of children, women, negroes, and Indians prove. The fear of the police and the workhouse restrained him.

One day, turning the corner of the post-office, he found a crowd of newsboys and shoeblacks gathered about something that seemed to give them great satisfaction. Impelled by curiosity, he struggled through the ring of urchins, and found in the middle a little neatly-dressed six-year-old being baited by the cruel fiends. The poor boy, frightened fearfully, stood pale and trembling in their midst, his little store of newspapers tumbled together at his feet. Ely was aroused. Swinging his box viciously around, leaving bloody marks on noses, he cried out, with more profanity than I care to record: "Give the kid a chance! give the kid a chance!"

This diversion brought on a general engagement, that a good natured policeman arrested.

"Stop yer fightin', ye dirty little devils, and don't disturb the public peace!" exclaimed the stout guardian of the peace and dignity of the commonwealth, as he knocked the contestants to the right and left.

The lad thus rescued clung to Rat Ely as his preserver. The Rat felt proud of his guardianship. Gathering up the fallen papers, he conducted his ward to a seat on the plaza, and consoled the boy by telling him not to be a spooney. The lad could not, however, recover from his scare, and begged his preserver to take him home. Ely, without concealing his contempt, complied. A long walk brought them to a rather handsome house, in a handsomely-built part of the city, and Ely would have parted with his ward at the foot of the stone steps leading to the front door, but the boy begged so hard to have him enter that he did so. The door was opened by a stout domestic in petticoats, who stared in amazement at the ragged newsboy. She made no comment, however. In the hall they met a little girl of about twelve, a bright-eyed, curly-headed miss, who exclaimed:

"Why, Arnold!" and her face expressed what her lips failed to, as she gazed at Arnold's companion.

"He saved my life, he did!" exclaimed the lad, "and I want mamma to thank him."

His mamma, thus appealed to, soon appeared. She was a woman of about thirty, in whose pale face were imprinted lines of grief and anxiety. She heard the story of how her little hopeful had started out to make a living for the family by selling papers. and how he had been set upon by bad boys, and would have been killed but for the interference of this dirty, much-coated little Samaritan. The good woman listened, as tears coursed their way down her pale cheeks, and then, to Ely's alarm and great embarrassment, caught him in her arms and kissed him. Rat had never been spoken to kindly. let alone being caressed, and he stood in pitiable trouble at the demonstration.

"Only to think," sobbed the mother, "of my angel going out to sell papers to get us bread, and you protected him! God bless

you." And then she put Ely to the question as to his home, life
and all. As he jerked out his short replies in awkward sentences,
her heart was still more stirred.

"No parents, no home, poor little fellow! t is dreadful," she
exclaimed, and then after a thoughtful pause, added : "You shall
have a shelter at least ; we are poor, and, God knows, suffering ;
but as long as *we* have a shelter you shall share it. What is your
name ?"

"Rat Ely," he responded.

"Oh no, not that ; that cannot be your name ?"

"Yes, it is though; ain't got no other."

"Well, Ely, you return here to-night, and I will have some
clothes for you, and you shall have a supper and a bed."

Rat Ely took all this without thanks. He had been so roughly
treated through life that such generosity seemed suspicious. He
looked inquiringly at the mother, then at the pretty girl from head
to foot, and having reached the lowest extremity, said :

"Shine 'em up !"

The mother smiled and the little girl laughed.

"No, my boy," the lady responded ; "but you may in the
morning—every morning if you will."

Thinking he had discovered the origin of the amazing proposition that gave him food and lodging, he got out of the house as
quickly as possible.

The kind Providence that yet works miracles in behalf of the
innocent and oppressed had brought our hero in contact with the
distressed and sorrowing family of Arnold Stevens. The agencies
prepared by unbelieving men had failed, but Christ, who promised
to be with us to the end of time, is still here. He gazes lovingly at
us through the mother's eye ; walks unseen under the humble
garb of the good Sister of Charity ; devotes a life to service and
privation ; cries out for mercy to the poor dumb brutes through
the heart of a Bergh ; on every hand testifies to the truth of His
promise to be with us to the end.

This strange disappearance of the one bread-winner had brought
not only the shame of slanderous tongues, but the distress of
clamorous creditors. "There is but one thing more cruel than a

million of dollars," said Senator Sprague, "and that is a million and a half."

Rat Ely returned, and quite alarmed the family by his voracious appetite, that threatened to clear the poor larder. The good hearted mother worked diligently all day in making him a new suit out of some old clothes of her lost husband, and a cot was given the lad in a room immediately under the roof.

When Ely came to don his new suit a grave trouble oppressed him. It afforded him no room for the concealment of his treasures. After some study he tore a hole in his mattress and hid book and flask therein. He was so unused to the ways of civilized life, that he did not know that a bed had to be rearranged every morning and the first bed-making by Bridget brought that honest and indignant domestic to Mrs. Stevens' room. Bridget had not approved of this charity on the part of a woman too poor to pay her wages, and she cried, with a red face :

"It's a dirty little sot and thafe yer harborin', ma'am ! Look what I found hid in his mattress."

Mrs Stevens did look, turning pale and trembling so that she could scarcely stand. It was her own Christmas gift to her husband, and through the stains of use and abuse could yet be traced the monogram painted upon the side. With trembling hands she seized the precious relic and looked at it through tears, until, to Bridget's astonishment and alarm, she fell fainting to the floor. All day long she sat with the flask in her hand. How slowly the hours wore away until evening brought Ely back to his supper and bed. Then she told him of her sad affliction, and begged to know how he got possession of the flask. The boy, in return, related his adventures ; more briefly and graphically told than I have been able to give them. When he ended she said :

"The book, Ely, the book."

"Got it !" he said, and hurrying to the dormitory, returned with what Bridget had failed to discover. Mrs. Stevens opened it and found the fortune for which her husband had probably lost his life.

Possessed of means, not only sufficient to relieve the irate creditors, but to employ men to trace her lost husband, she again con-

sulted the detectives.   These able men, who figure so prominently
in fiction, listened incredulously to the story.   However, as money
was to be had to pay expenses, and a reward of $5000 was offered
for success in working out the mystery, the miraculously endowed
detectives—endowed, I mean, in novels and plays—went to work.
The detective of literature is a wonderful man.   He is a Fouche
and a Bucket rolled in one ; who, to great honesty, adds a wisdom
th.t makes the reader hold his breath.   In real life, he is a fellow
who fails as a thief, and turns detective that he may share the
plunder without fear of punishment.

Mrs. Stevens soon learned that, to accomplish her purpose, she
would have to take control.   The head detective proved ineffably
stupid, and made his stupidity offensive by his conceit.   Little Ely
volunteered to show the police from the river the place where Mr.
Stevens left him and was landed.   The wise detectives treated the
proposition with contempt.   But the wife accepted, and a party
was made up to row in an open boat down the river.   Ely sat in
the bow of the boat, looking out eagerly, w thout any misgivings
as to the accuracy of his lead.   It was no light task.   The river,
familiar enough to the lad at the city, was an unknown region below, and the change, from a terrible flood to an ordinary stage,
was so great that he might well be puzzled.   The brain, however,
that has not been obscured by book learning, and the eyes not
dulled by reading, take. up and retain all of this material world
they encounter, and, at a point in their progress, the little fellow
threw up his h nd and cried, "Here' the place !"

The boat was he ded to the bank, and the search began.   Everybody living along the shore, and all within a mile in the country
back, were questioned.   It was slow and tedious work, and without
eliciting a particle of information.   All seemed dead, blank ignorance.   The se rch was render d irritating by the conduct of the
detective.   He was sullen and inattentive.

"You seem to be without hope," said Mrs. Stevens.   The man
shook his head in assent.   "Well," continued the wife, "what do
you think ?"

"I don't want to discourage you, mum," replied the creature ;
"but it's wild-goose, all uv it."

"What is wild-goose?"

"A follerin' this little thievin' cove. Now, biz is biz, an' it's my biz to speak out. It's all plain to me, for I ain't a woman, an's my heart don't blind my sense, I see it."

"What do you see?"

"The gent is tumbled senseless off uv the *Helen Marr.* He is caught in a tree. This little cove is a-sailin' down on a raft—all likely. Well, he just helps himself to the valuables, and lets the body go ; an' now he 'eads ye a wild-goose chase, on a shore where ye see nobody knows nothin'. Oh, I'm up to these wharf-rats. They are as cunnin' as Satan, an' can lie like sin."

The poor woman at this brutal speech, made in the presence of the lad, felt at first dismayed, and then, glancing at his indignant face, had her confidence restored. Crowding down the pain and disgust, she said quietly :

"That is harder to believe than his story. This river gives up its dead, and had the body of my poor husband been carried off on this great highway, it would have been discovered sooner or later, and the newspapers filled with the fact. No, the boy tells the truth. We will search from here to the city, and from here south, until he is found. You take whichever direction you please. This lad and I will take the other. I pay you for your time. Which way will you go ?"

"Well, mum, if you will, you will. If the gent did get to shore alive, he uv course made for home."

" No, he didn't !" cried Ely.

" Why not ?" asked the detective, contemptuously.

"Coz he'd a-got there 'fore this."

T e detective grunted. It was arranged that he should continue the search in the direction of the city, while the wife and Ely went south. The detective obeyed by walking to the nearest railway station, scorning to ask another question, and so returned to the city and his associate thieves and beer.

The unhappy wife procured a conveyance and slowly and wearily continued her sad quest. She not only questioned at every house, but sought the country doctors and undertakers on the way —this for days, but all without avail Had the earth opened and swallowed her husband on his reaching shore, he could not have more entirely and suddenly disappeared.

All this time the words of the detective were working at her heart. She gazed earnestly at the boy, and again and again made him tell over his story, hoping yet fearing to find some contradiction upon which to base a doubt. But the little fellow never varied. Her husband could not be dead ; death makes an event in a quiet community. It is known of all men, and goes to the record of memory, if not to print. Yet where could he be ?

At last she caught a clue. A woman, bending over a washtub in a farm-house near the river, being interrogated, said:

" Ain't hearn tell of any sick man. But there is a sick feller as was took off the river in the big flood, lyin' very poorly at the Widder Tuckerman's."

" Where, where is that ? " asked the wife, eagerly.

" Well, nigh on to a mile from here. The man what had the poor cretur in a wagin couldn't get anybody to take him till Doctor Olds hit the percession, and he pursuaded the widder to take him. She is grevin' for her man, that was drowned in that same flood, and felt more like doin' somethin' for the poor cretur."

" He is sick ! " exclaimed the wife, motioning the driver to move on, and then, catching her breath and his hand, stopped him to get the reply.

" Well, yes, mity poorly and flighty—keeps up a great talk about nothin' and sumthin' along at the same time—tho' I did see the doctor goin' by yesterday, and he allowed there was a turn."

Along the rough road the carriage was hurried, until the humble home of the widow was reached. It was well for the patient that Mrs. Stevens met the old doctor at the door. To him she hurriedly told her story. The physician listened patiently to the end, and then said:

"Your husband has been very ill of brain fever. He is yet hanging doubtfully to life, but is better. Glad you have come, for he nee's nursing." Without another word, he led the way to the sick-room.

The appearance of the sick man shocked the wife, and made

her for a moment doubt the identity. Stretched upon a rude bed, under the glare o. curtainless windows, lay an emaciated form with such a ghastly pale face, pinched features, and cavernous eyes, that her heart stilled its beating, and she nearly fainted. Love, through tears, found recognition, and, woman·like, the wife turned instantly to nurse. The go d old doctor, in a whisper, called her attention to the fact that he was sleeping quietly, and said that in this, his first natural sleep, was promise of health. He hoped that with waking would come reason.

So it proved. After a long, long sleep the patient opened his eyes, and, recognizing his wife, whispered, "Darling." With tears falling on his wasted face, she kissed him, and then remembering the warning of the doctor, put her finger to her lips with a reproving nod, and went about her silent work of restoration.

Arnold Stevens' fine constitution, aided by skimmed milk and tender nursing, grew strong apace. Some days after, with his poor head resting on his wife's bosom, he told, in broken fragments, of his misfortunes. He had evidently been followed from Pennsylvania by men bent on robbing him. When he left the card-table to get his overcoat, he went from the stateroom through the door upon the guard, which, as the boat rounded to, would fetch him nearest the landing. Hearing the door close, the robbers ran round, and while one, as he thought, seized his valise, supposing it had his valuables, the other struck him on the head, and the three threw him into the river.

"A ragged little fellow," he continued, "pulled me out of the water."

"Yes, yes," said his wife, "I know that ; but afterward, when those bad men took you from the raft, what happened?"

The husband looked surprised at this interruption, and then continued : "I quarrelled with them for leaving the poor lad. I called them miserable brutes, and when we reached the shore I was knocked senseless for my epithets. I don't know how long I lay there, but when I recovered my senses, I had been robbed of my watch, pocketbook, overcoat and all my papers. Some hours after a stout fellow rowed by, and, hailing him, I offered him fifty dollars to row me after the raft and rescue the lad. I was half

crazy, for the poor boy had my bonds. I suppose I became unconscious, for I knew no more until I opened my eyes here on you,
dear wife." After a pause, he asked, anxiously : " Did that man
find the lad ?" She shook her head, and, with a deep sigh, he went
on : "Poor little fellow and poor me ! You get your miserable
husband again, Pet, but you get a ruined man."

"Oh no, not quite that," she laughed ; "the little fellow
found himself, and, what is more to the purpose, he found me,
with all your wealth. Ely ! Ely ! come here."

The husband started up in amazement as the little fellow
ran in.

"God bless you !" cried Mr. Stevens, putting his emaciated
hand on the round head. "You shall be my boy after this."

It is a melancholy fact that the Rat received this benediction
and promise with solemn indifference. The emotions of sensibil-
ity are the result of culture, and the Rat had not yet been taught
and trained to that luxury.

THE FEMALE CLERK AT WASHINGTON.

THE "Department" at Washington is a cross between West Point and the penitentiary. It has all the discipline and degradation of the one, and the despotism of the other. Filled with workers from the political fields, who have gotten places for services at the polls through the influence of politicians, and as their offices are held subject to the selfish wants of the patrons, the laborers live in constant horror of dismissal. The rod held over them is more potent and cruel than was the whip of the overseer on the Southern plantations.

To make more clear the despotism, there is no part of the civilized world in which the iron law of caste has such firm foundation and such immovable power. The President of the United States to a "Department" is a god in whose presence clerks must stand with heads bared, and speak when spoken to with bated breath. After him comes the Cabinet officer, and as he stalks along the corridors, head up and form composed, with a look that glares from his face, flashes from his step, and waves majestically from his very coat-tails, a silence precedes and follows him, like that which pervades a grove when an old hen-hawk goes swooping through. All the little birds suspend their singing until the feathered pirate is gone. How the messengers bow down in the humility of mannered prayer as they swing open the heavy doors to this incarnation of official flummery!

After the Secretary appears the Senator. The Senator carries a heavier pressure of official dignity to the square inch than even the Cabinet officer. But he does not get such an awful and imposing recognition as that "tin-god-on-wheels" known as the head of the Department.

The Member of the House comes next. He mars his dignity

through his hurry ; a steam-tug cannot pose as a seventy-four. Then the average member chews tobacco, and this use of the weed indicates human weakness. True official dignity calls for a sub-limated, godlike condition of fog that lifts one above common human wants and weaknesses. The late George Washington, as seen by the multitude, emblems a Department notion of true greatness.

After the Member of the House appears the Head of a Bureau. Great Scott! what an immense creature he is in his own estima-tion. Now, next to being immense in the mind of others, the best thing is to be gigantic in your own.

And so file in the captains of thousands, and captains of hun-dreds, until the poor, wretched clerks appear, living on a bare sub-sistence, and not able to sleep of nights lest this be taken from them. The misery of the place comes from the uncertain tenure of office. The male clerks are mostly men unfitted by nature for the fierce competition of human life. This drove them in the first instance into politics, and from thence they drift into the De-partments. Originally helpless, they mould into deformities, and expulsion from office means starvation.

The tenure is uncertain because every new member fetches to Washington a fresh following to be provided for, and he is fierce in his demands. The new civil service rules are meant to mitigate this evil. The trouble with them is that they are based on false premises. The Hon. Eaton, of Connecticut, and the Hon. Pen-dleton, of Ohio, a politician I christened some years since by the name he is now known by, "Gentleman George," copied this competitive system from the English Government, where the service suffered from being monopolized by the aristocracy, and all the places were filled with incompetent younger sons and depend-ents. To rid the Government of this, and throw the positions open, the competitive examination was instituted.

Now the trouble with us is, not in the lack of ability, but in the absence of honesty, the poor pay, and the uncertain tenure of office. An official with us has to steal to live and that rapidly, in view of the uncertainty of official life.

The English competitive nonsense is, with us, the mere shifting of responsibility, or rather the appearance of it, from the appointing power to the board, and the board is accommodating. It comprehends the force of a wink.

However, I am not engaged in treating on civil service, but to illustrate it in the story of Miss Alice Doehead a would-be female clerk at Washington.

Hon. Daniel Doehead was a wealthy man, who bought a seat in the Senate, very much as his wife bought her carriage, to enhance his social position. A quiet, inoffensive, solid man, he filled his place as a butter-firkin would have done—no more, no less. He looked to the committee for instructions, and followed his leader in his votes, and so glided quietly along the well-oiled tracks of legislation.

In the same way the family, consisting of wife and daughter, assumed its place in society. Renting the gorgeously furnished house of a retired Cabinet official, the Hon. Doehead gave dinners, and Mrs. D. receptions. The roll of carriages and the crowd of visitors told in the usual way of their social success. Alice, the lovely little daughter, shy as a fawn, shone as a belle, and, for the two seasons given the family, had in train suitors, running from the bald headed widowed Senators down to Dick Wingate, her father's private secretary, a handsome young fellow, who had lifted himself from a thousand-dollar clerk to a twenty-five hundred dollar secretary, through, first, his knowledge of short-hand, and, secondly, his power to supply the brain necessary to make the phonographic skill available. He loved the little Alice, but dared not say so ; and she, regarding the secretary as the handsomest and most fascinating of men, treated him, on that account, with extreme reserve.

The political world has forgotten—for the political world is as short of memory as it is short of principle—how a vacancy once occurred in the Senate by the sudden death of the Hon. Doehead. The remote cause of his demise was attributed to the Washington malaria that, born of the Kidwell bottoms, is said to float over the national Capitol and kill the solons. The fact is that the fatal malaria did not float at all. It is in perpetual solution and well bottled. It is composed of cheap champagne and doctored whiskey, and kills on sight. The Hon. Doehead not only disappeared from earth, but his riches went with him. The poor wife, who had been kept in ignorance all her married life of her husband's affairs, awakened to the dismal fact that she and her daughter were without a cent on which to live.

While casting about for a refuge from their poverty, the daughter thought of and suggested a clerkship at Washington. The suggestion was acted on, and so wretchedly poor were they that a sale of their personal effects only gave them money enugh to reach the national capital.

They arrived in a vacation of Congress, when the wide, hot city seemed to be sleeping without even the disturbing noise of a snore. The street cars, running empty, alone awakened, with their rattle, the echoes of the deserted streets. At the hotels, that superior being, the head clerk. rested like a volcano in repose ; nothing but the dazzling gleam of his diamond bosom indicating the fearful power that lies hid in the awful explosion of the word "Front," when he consigns the wretch of a guest to the hands of a call-boy.

Mother and daughter did not disturb the repose of this superior person, but found refuge in a humble room located on Boundary Street, and immediately went forth to seek the means of livelihood. The Administration was absent. At the Executive mansion the servants alone lounged about its lofty rooms, and through its lofty windows the pungent odors of the Kidwell bottoms wafted to and fro. At the Departments, in the cool corridors, the messengers, tilted back in easy chairs, dozed undisturbed. Two of the Cabinet alone remained at their posts. These were patriotic, conscientious officials, who could not consent to vacate their positions while certain heavy contracts were being executed. Some vile calumniators insinuated that these officials were personally concerned in the millions involved, by asserting as much in the columns of journals, under huge head-lines. But no one heeded their libels ; and, although these high officials were subsequently dismissed from place, and one of them indicted, they yet bid fair to die lamented, and leave memories sweet to the mind of the American multitude that piously refrains from speaking ill of the dead while heaping vast oceans of abuse on the living.

The poor women, walking in from their distant home, trailed wearily from Department to Department in vain. The two Cabinet officials, who had partaken of their hospitality in their prosperous hours, received them politely, one each, and after that it was found impossible to gain the presence of either. Hour after hour they sat in the ante-chamber of the one or the other, and saw hard-looking men and bold women admitted and dismissed, but their turn never came. They had no political influence, that open sesame to the cave of the forty thieves, and our Saviour himself without this might have starved in the ante-chamber of a Government official.

As time wore on their few clothes wore out, especially the shoes, and their little store of money got less and less. At last, reduced to one pair of shoes, and a few crackers each day, that they moistened with tears, the shy little girl was forced to go alone, the mother remaining at home, having nothing to put on her feet. The poor girl lengthened her walk by a square to avoid a certain bake-shop, not that, like Dick Swiveller, she had a debt there, but to avoid the odor of the place that fairly maddened her. She thought of her old friend and father's secretary, Dick Wingate, but found that he was off with a Senatorial committee appointed to put in the summer junketing in the North.

There was one hope alone left mother and daughter. The Secretary of the Department devoted to Jobs and Expenditures had been not only the warm personal friend of the late Senator, but the Senator had been actively instrumental in elevating the Secretary to his high and responsible position. He was away from the capital, but expected back every day.

At last the great man arrived, and Alice was ushered into his presence. It was an imposing presence in every sense of the word. He was tall, broad-shouldered, full-stomached, and needed only two ram's horns to make him a living representative of the dead satyr sung of in Greek mythology. His coarse face, full of animal feeling, was so without intellect that a wicked Sunday journal let fly at him an epigram that read :

"In Goldsmith's day there once a wonder grew,
 How one small head could carry all it knew ;
 But now 'tis changed, we here a wonder find,
 To see so large a carcass, with so little mind."

Nature is considerate, and gave to the huge Secretary a cunning that more than compensated for an absence of intellect.

The huge animal received Alice with gushing cordiality. Indeed he held her little hand in his much longer than the occasion
called for, and gazed into her delicate, lovely face with an inten-
sity of expression that made the poor maiden drop her eyes and
blush, she scarcely knew why. He promised her an immediate
place, took her address, and, to the confusion of the two women,
dashed up to the door of their humble abode, and insisted on
their ridi·g with him to the Soldiers' Home. Both could not go,
for one would be in her stockings, and Alice was consigned to his
fatherly care.

The ride was not pleasant to Alice, for, in the first place, she
was famishing, actually sick and dizzy from lack of food ; in the
second place, the great man's conversation and manner were unpleasant. He dwelt upon her beauty, her old lovers, and insisted
upon holding her hand. Alice was young and confiding, but not
altogether inexperienced, for two seasons in Washington had forced
much on her mind that had given her knowledge without affecting
her purity. The ride, at last, came to an end and was followed
by a supper at Welcher's. The poor girl tried hard to restrain
herself, but hunger was too much for her, and she was ashamed of
the fierce appetite she exhibited. The Secretary did not eat. but
did drink enormously, and was immensely amused at his little
friend's enjoyment. She ate all offered her, but refused the prof-
fered wine.

"Your mother looks delicate, Alice." He was very familiar,
this great man. "The grief at the loss of your dear father and
my dear friend is telling on her ; she needs delicacies and some of
this old wine. I must see that she has quails and some old sherry.
We will start now." He gave an order that Alice feebly resisted,
and a basket, well laden, was placed in the carriage and left with
Alice at her home.

Poor Mrs. Doehead thanked God upon her knees that night long and earnestly for thus sending this great and good man to their relief. It may have been our heavenly Father who sent him, but Alice was distressed. There was something in it that made her pure white soul feel, to say the least, uneasy, and when she prayed it was to the holy Mary, Mother of God, to protect the orphan and the widow.

I have not the space nor the inclination to dwell upon what followed in the continued and unremitting favor of this good man. It is true he gave Alice no clerkship, but the rides continued. The supply of delicacies and wines went on ; and one day the great Secretary, while excusing himself for not finding the place he desired, insisted on loaning the widow some money, to be repaid from the girl's salary when she secured the position he had in view.

The summer wore on, and as autumn came in with its cool sea breezes from the Potomac, Washington seemed to wake up from its sleepy recess. Alice noticed, in her rides, the increased number of gay equipages they met, and she was also forced to note the strange stare the occupants gave her as. nodding to the Secretary, they swept by. Once or twice she caught the gleam of a smile that flashed like sheet-lightning over faces that had greeted the Secretary, after the carriages had passed.

There is no city on earth where the tide of human life changes so rapidly and completely as at Washington. It is true there is a population of old families, and it marries, has children, and lives and dies as elsewhere ; but it is not upon the surface. It lives unseen, and deep sea-soundings are necessary to bring specimens to the surface. Now a new world of faces came sweeping into Washington, as Alice saw it ; but there was enough of a remnant left to teach the child a lesson. There were people who had partaken of her father's generous hospitality in their more prosperous hour, and had. many of them, followed. flattered, sought, and sued the little heiress. Now they gazed at her with cold. averted faces and so all the world was strange.

The cruelest blow came when the long-looked-for Dick Wingate, the handsome, genial, clever young man, whose manner had told her instinctively that he loved, although no vow of love had ever passed his lips. I say the blow came when he returned. Alice met him upon the street, and she could not refrain from hurrying her steps and holding out her hands with a sunny smile. What was her amazement, her distress, at receiving from him only a cold bow, and no notice of her outstretched hands as he passed. Her heart and breath seemed to forsake her, and as the one came back through a sob, the other seemed to bound back as if struck with a blow. What could it mean? Why should he, too, turn on her?

She did not know that, hearing of the family misfortunes, and her return to Washington, the young man had hurried, with his heart in his mouth, to the Capitol as soon as his official duties would permit; and that on his arrival all his loving hopes were blighted by the cruel scandal that met him at every turn. Scandal is the moral miasma of Washington that touches all, and taints all it touches. Common report made his little love the mistress of a man (his own chief, for Dick was his private secretary), whose very presence was pollution to womanhood.

She did not know this, of course; she would have died of shame and mortification had the slightest whisper reached her ear. Nor did he know that his cruel blow had driven her to the edge of the precipice over which he believed she had already fallen. The Hon. Secretary, madly infatuated, had been cunningly careful not to frighten the timid fawn he meant to sacrifice. He had, it is true, done all in his power to compromise the girl, well knowing that when reputation is lost a great safeguard is broken down, and desperation accomplishes what passionate appeals fail to win. To this end he had sent his carriage at midnight to the corner of the block upon which the helpless women lived— a neighborhood of clerks, where rowdies out late or police out early could see it drive away.

Let no one believe for a moment that I am romancing. That fact last told was notorious in Washington when our Government reached. let us hope, its lowest plane of pollution—a level that made the most shameful and shameless periods of European court-life both refined and respectable.

While Alice remained innocent, her womanly instincts kept her warned, and although the social and political world was busy with her name, she had kept the wrong-doer at arm's distance. He had passed from rides and suppers to gifts and notes, all the while holding out the promise of immediate place that was never given. Returning home after the cruel cut from her old associate and lover, crowding down as best she might the grief that had made her wild and desperate, she found a note from her patron, asking her to come to his house at five that afternoon. At any other time she would have declined this meeting. But now as she was, she resolved to comply; the consequences of such a step dimly shadowed themselves upon her maidenly fears, but she thrust them aside. There was the one man of all the world who had taken pity on them, saved them from starvation, and stood ready to give her an honest and honorable calling; so she complied.

Ascending the broad stone steps of the then most aristocratic mansion of Washington, she rang the bell, and the huge door swung open immediately, the Secretary himself ushered the little girl into his library. The wide, lofty hall, dimly lit, exhibited a wealth of art and upholstery such as Alice had nearly forgotten in her banishment from luxury to privation. In the superbly-adorned library she was somewhat startled to find the daylight shut out, and the beautiful room lighted by a lamp on the library table that made heavy shadows on all sides.

The presence of innocent maidenhood awed the selfish brute. He found it difficult, although fortified with wine, to advance in his purpose. Seating himself, he said that in the absence of his family he kept but one servant, and the fellow had taken a holiday to himself. He went on to say that he could not consent to have the lovely daughter of his dear old friend placed in a miserable position, and had made up his mind to share with Alice and her mother some of the wealth it had been his fortune to acquire. He wanted to be a protector to her, and surround her with all the luxury to which she had been so accustomed. She should live with her mother in a lovely little house, servants at will, and the loveliest little *coupé* to be had for money, and all he asked in return was her love.

He approached as he spoke, and she rose from her chair, shocked and frightened, now that the fact of degradation was frankly presented to her. She drew back, pale and trembling; but the creature had gone too far to retreat, and seizing her in his arms he attempted kisses that came to her face heavy with whiskey and tobacco. She struggled to free herself, and failing, screamed out a piteous appeal.

"Oh, let me go!" she screamed ; "oh, for God's sake, let me go. I cannot, I cannot——"

Further resistance was suppressed in his embraces, and as she freed her face she gave utterance to a wild despairing cry, the Hon. Secretary felt an iron grip at his throat, and before he could realize the interruption, he was hurled over a sofa, and, striking his head upon a projection of the library shelves, fell stunned to the floor. Alice had fainted, and Dick Wingate stood for a second between the two. Seizing a glass of water, he proceeded to revive the little girl, and having succeeded, looked over his shoulder to see the Hon. Secretary in a sitting position with the blood streaming from his wounded head. Had the great sovereign State of —— that delighted to honor her favorite son seen his plight and position, doubt'ess great sympathy would have been felt. The favorite son of a sovereign State, continuing in his recumbent position upon the floor, let loose his opinion of his private secretary in language more profane than polite.

Dick Wingate would have responded, and continued the general engagement then and there, but for a faint appeal from the rescued maiden to take her thence, which caused him to lift her from her chair and leave the house. That he escorted her home, that he soothed her troubled soul with loving words that were received and in a manner returned, followed of course.

The next morning Wingate, private secretary to this lofty chief, received a summons from his master and responded promptly. Wingate thought of his providential interference with great comfort to himself. He remembered coming unexpectedly to the Secretary, into the city ; he had hurried with his report to the house, and, finding the bell unheeded, had let himself in with his latch-key, and, moving along the noiseless carpet of the lofty hall, had been a witness to all that passed.

Dick found his chief in a woful plight, with his head bandaged and his eyes indicating a sleepless night. He expected from the Secretary a torrent of abuse and instant dismissal. To the youth's surprise, he was received pleasantly and invited to seat himself.

"Dick," said the Secretary, after a pause, "you did me a favor yesterday. You saved me from an awful scrape. The fact is, my boy, I had been drinking Tom Lapham's whiskey. Tom's whiskey does not make a man drunk, it makes him crazy. You did right to knock me down, and I wish you had gone on and given me a damned thrashing. You can do so yet. I believe it would relieve me from this mean feeling. Kick me! Dick; kick me!"

The proposition was so grotesque that the lover, greatly rejoiced to find the girl of his heart innocent, could not help laughing.

"You have the laugh Dick; you have the laugh," continued the high official, "and it hurts more than the blow. It won't do, my boy, for you to remain here You will be a continual reproach to me. There is a place vacant in Dakota, good for $6000 a year, with the *perquisites*, Dick; healthy *perquisites*, my boy. Go, and God bless you!"

Dick Wingate accepted the position, and soon left Washington for his distant post. Before doing so, a little sacrament at St. Matthew's Church made Alice his wife; and, kneeling at the altar, the beautiful bride returned her prayerful thanks from her heart to the Blessed Virgin for protection through perilous trials.

THE GREAT DYNAMITE SCARE.

NOVEL XIII.

THERE is no superstition so well fixed in the popular mind that is so unfounded as that which prevails under the phrase of "national traits." Humanity is about the same the world over. and the modification which comes of climate. different pursuits and races, is so slight that it leaves man very much as nature made him. The dude Absalom of Israel is the dude of to-day. and the brutal man-killer worshipped in the barbarous ages is the same man killer we bury in glory in this afternoon of the nineteenth century.

Nevertheless, we continue to ascribe to the German, as a national characteristic, honest simplicity, that no facts to the contrary can disturb

Diedrich Von Cott, of Von Cott & Co., Soap and Candles, came in this way to be regarded as an amiable and guileless old gentleman, whose word was better than an average man's bond. This came of the fact that he was a stout man, of full, round stomach, and a genial, round, red face, reminding one of the Western song which said :

> When he lived, he lived in clover,
> And when he died, he died all over.

Only the line should read, "When he laughed he laughed all over." A smile would spread o'er his broad face as a batter cake spreads on a griddle, and then a subterranean agitation would seem to disturb his huge paunch, and extend to all parts of him—out to his chubby fingers and down to his fat toes.

The curious part of it was that this manifestation of humor seemed to be of a physical origin. In his intellectual processes, Diedrich was without any sense of humor. The fact is, that part of his get-up was singularly serious. His money getting, for example, had no shade of fun in it. He gave to profit and loss the keen-eyed attention of serious thought. There was no laughter over business. Had it been otherwise, he would not have built up a vast trade out of an humble beginning—from a shop that a stout man could have run a stick through, and, shouldering up, march off with. From this small beginning, Diedrich progressed until it represented a million in capital, a manufacturing concern that made a village of some hundreds of workmen, and so well out of debt that the hard times seemed to leave the concern undisturbed.

Yet Diedrich laughed through life. He could even laugh over a joke at his own expense, and his associates had one that they never tired putting at him, and he never failed in his earthquake of merriment in response. The joke was this : One day the old gentleman stumbled over a box of candles, and went down a flight of steps to the basement of his storehouse in a way that made his clerks and workmen believe that the head of the firm had split all to pieces. He was picked up. if I may use such an expression of a man weighing two hundred and twenty-six, but could not be set on end. The stout workmen deposited their damaged boss in his carriage, and from his carriage to his bed.

"Ah ! mine frau," he said, with some profanity I do not record, "I'm kil'd in mine pack." The German physician called in found no bones broken, nor could he discover any internal injury ; so he bound up the old gentleman's head and put him on active treatment of whiskey and water. The one he applied externally, the other was poured down his throat.

A few weeks after, the great manufacturer of Arnold's "light and grace"—I mean grease—rose from his bed to a sofa, and, in course of time, to his feet. But in the pedal extremity a new trouble manifested itself. Diedrich's big toe of his right foot was so swollen and sore he could not walk. Again the German doctor made a diagnosis, and pronounced it gout. The burly patient was treated for that aristocratic disorder. He was put on low diet, which he violated whenever his wife's back was turned and his daughter Catrina had an opportunity to obey her father's wink and surreptitiously give him all sorts of indigestible food. Of course he grew no better, rather worse, and, propped up in one arm chair he had his leg, fearfully bandaged, on another, while his temper got to be something awful.   Using his crutch as a weapon, offensive and defensive, he had the servants dodging about him to avoid the pokes and blows, or off in their rooms bathing each other's bruises with arnica.

The German physician brought in other German doctors, and the solemn conclave smoked and sputtered over the irritable patient until he drove them all out.

"Mine frau !" he cried, " ve mid Catrina to Europe goes, py tam, und consulds mid doctors vot knows someting.   Dose vellers is jakasses."

To Europe they sailed, and from Europe he returned with his afflicted wife and daughter, the ailing toe in a worse condition than when they left our shores.   Diedrich was not only losing his genial disposition, but he was losing flesh.   IIis cheeks lost color, and his skin hung loose as his clothes.   One day, a little Hebrew horse-doctor, a great friend of Diedrich's, while talking to the old gentleman, asked to see the gouty part.   The bandages were unrolled, very much with the pride that Dogberry boasted his losses, or a boy shows another boy his stone-bruise.   The son of Moses looked long and earnestly at the swollen and inflamed member.   Suddenly. without a word of warning, he seized with a frightful grip of his right hand the swollen toe, and threw his entire weight and strength in one pull at the member.   Old Diedrich uttered a yell to which that of the wild Indians or the armed Confederates was a mere infant.

"Oh, mine Cot ! mine Cot !" he gasped, "you kil'd me !" And he made a pass at the little Hebrew with his crutch that would have ended then and there the valuable life of a veterinary surgeon had not that child of Israel dodged the blow.

" Mine friend," said the Hebrew, calmly, from the further side of the room, " your dam't old toe vas oud ov joint."

So it proved.   In a few weeks the old gentleman was on his stout legs, as well as ever.   From that out, it was the thing for all of Mr. Von Cott's friends and associates to ask him gravely about his gout. He would respond : " It is petter as vell," and then the laughter would follow, no one enjoying it more than Diedrich himself.

The great bulk of Diedrich & Co.'s wealth came from the "Co." The "Co." was a thin, angular, misbegotten son of man, who had discovered or invented a cheap soap that was fair to look at, sweet to smell, and bound to remove the dirt if it took the skin. There was one fact generally recognized, and that was that old Fakin, the inventor, never tried the soap upon himself. As he grew rich, he bought a huge diamond, and when he put on full dress it consisted simply in placing this head-light of a locomotive in his dirty shirt-bosom. No one knew when the "Co." was born. I doubt whether any one ever inquired. This was before the newspapers went into the production of hideous cuts from their cheap process that pillory everybody, and make the subject writhe in anguish, and one's family and friends fairly howl in wrath. Had Fakin survived to this day. he would have had his face, that was ugly enough to scare horses, adorning the fifty columns of the New York *World*, and two-thirds of the readers would have passed it with a glance of horror as the head of an assassin or Jay Gould.

A solitary. miserly man, of no emotions beyond the accumulation of money, the "Co." one day took old Diedrich's breath by proposing to marry Catrina, his partner's only child. Had he suggested to the father that the two should walk hand-in-hand to the centre of the Brooklyn Bridge and then jump off, he could not have been more astonished. But how is that about "Sin," that we first decline an introduction to and end by embracing? In the same way Von Cott had come to regard the "Co." This Sin-on-legs had grown familiar—in a business way, it is true—but it had paved the way to the matrimonial proposition ; and the senior, after recovering from the shock, began to think that it would not be a bad arrangement after all. He had been worried over Fakin's getting out of the business as much as he did. and now the way was open. He told Fakin he would refer the matter to Catrina, and he did.

This "sole heiress of his house and heart" had bloomed into a German angel, such as Rubens was wont to paint. One, at first glance, was struck with her large blue eyes and white little teeth. Then came the delicate to notice complexion. in which the peach seemed to tinge the purest cream, while her hair was light, silken, and soft.   Her figure was voluptuous without being coarse, and altogether the little girl had a right to rule her fond old father, for she was so cunning in her ways, as well as beautiful in his sight.

When the paternal Diedrich came to consider his rash promise to submit the proposition to his daughter, he was not altogether certain as to how it would be received.   At last, however, he screwed his courage to the sticking-point, and said :

"Catrina ! mine pardner, Fakin, lubs you !"

"Well, mine fadder !" responded the little girl, imitating his broken English.   "I am glad he loves something besides his money."

"Mine chile, he me asks dot you marry mid him."

The girl opened her beautiful blue eyes and broke into an uncontrollable fit of laughter, in which, vainly endeavoring to restrain himself, the father joined.

"Well," she said, recovering her speech, "you tell Mr. Fakin that I am much obliged, and if he really wants a wife I'll speak a good word for him to the Widow Borgman."

Again a merry peal rang out, in which the old man joined with a tumultuous shaking of his stomach, until there was danger to the buttons of his vest.

"Vell, vell, Catrina, I dells him, but, mine chile, I gets old burty soon, and you must a husband have burty soon, too, eh ?"

"Yes, mine fadder," she said, sitting upon his knee, and putting her arms about his neck, "I have been thinking of that."

"Ah, you little rogue, you aboud dat tinks, eh ?" he said, fondly stroking her silken hair.

"Yes, and I was going to tell you this very day.   I promised Tom I would."

"Vas?   Tom !—vot, Catrina ?"

"I mean that Tom Slater loves me, and I love him, and we're going to be married."

"Catrina, you preaks your old fadder's heart—vot you say I cannot mine ears pelieve—Tom Slater ! dot veller vot works mine vactory in ?"

"Yes, indeed, and he's just the handsomest, cleverest, and best fellow in the world."

"Catrina !" said her father solemnly, as he put her from him, "Catrina ! you dot veller drops already. Mine Cot ! mine Catrina marry such vellers as dot !"

" Why, father, you began in that way—you know you did, and Tom's just as good as we are—and I love him—and—and, if you don't let us marry, I'll—I'll—kill myself." And the girl began to weep.

" Catrina, Catrina ! you stops dot. You ish vun grand lady, mid money, eber so much monies. You, a vorkman in mine vactory marry mid Catrina ! If dot veller comes mine house round, I hid mid a shtick !"

The little Catrina knew the paternal author of her being well enough to be satisfied that he was not only in earnest about this, but that any attempt to move him from his resolve would be in vain. He was amiable in all small things, but obstinate as a mule in matters when he made up his mind to be firm.

The little girl managed to meet her lover and report the sad result of her interview. The place of meeting was not poetic, being in the store-room, amid great piles of boxes, containing the Wonderful Soap and the Superior Candles. But Tom looked enough handsome to make up for all lost in that direction. He was a tall, square-shouldered good looking young man, and. under his paper cap and blue-flannel shirt, would have won the heart of Oscar Wilde.

" Well, frauline, are you going to throw me over for old Skeezicks ?" Tom asked.

Catrina had inherited something of her father's firmness, and she said "she'd die first." Tom sealed the vow with a long Abbott-kiss on her lovely mouth, that she held up to him with an inno-cent faith of a Mather's abandon that makes her *Juliet* so fascinating.

" I say, Catrina, my kitten," cried Tom, "if you'll stand by me, and do as I want you, we'll fetch the old bird round in no time."

Catrina promised, and then followed a long confidential talk, that ended with the little girl returning to her carriage, holding a knowing smile upon her lovely face, while Tom returned to the counting-room with a grin that he punctuated with no end of winks and finger-snapping, that made old Fakin stare, and the clerks believe that Tom had been indulging in liquor.

About that time the city was disturbed by certain socialist demonstrations of a most unpleasant sort to the solid men, who were singularly prejudiced against any other treatment of property than that which pertained to their possession. This culminated in the explosion of some dynamite bombs under bay-windows that shattered a large amount of plate-glass and scared a truck horse, an experienced and aged animal, to such an extent that he fell down, and although much urged by an efficient police refused positively to get up again. I believe the efforts of the efficient police ended in setting this aged animal on his legs again. Nothing was ever known as to the origin of this explos'on save a significant wink and a solemn shake of the head by O'Donovan Rossa, which cleared the great Irish patriot of any suspicion as to his having any hand in the violence.

The corpulent Diedrich shared with the other solid men a prejudice against such unseemly conduct. But his disgust was intensified, not long after, by receiving an anonymous letter, not only written in red ink, in which he was denounced as a " bloody bondholder, doomed to death," but adorned with an awful picture of a skull and cross-bones, over a cut of a very fat man swung up by the neck. The miserable soap and candle-maker affected to regard this as "dam't foolishness," but his hands trembled, while the red left all of his face, save and except his corpulent nose, that seemed to deepen in color while the alarm lasted.

Catrina seemed more alarmed than any one else, and begged her dear father to send the wretches all his bonds, and not to move from house or store without a body-guard, in the person of the valiant and active Tom Slater. The old gentleman pooh-poohed ! both propositions. But, terror seized him the day after, when he went to shave in the morning, and found another missive, skull and cross-bones, suspended fat man and all, beneath his shaving-glass. After that he could not open his paper, or turn down the sheets of his bed, without encountering this awful warning, and he began to think seriously of Catrina's advice, as to a body-guard.

The troubled mind of the worthy old gentleman turned him at

last to the handsome Tom, who readily undertook the guardianship of the threatened man. As there seemed to be no let-up in the terrible threats, Mr. Von Cott clung to his protector in the most confiding manner.

One evening, after a pleasant little dinner-party, at which the amorous Fakin appeared in full dress—that is, with his diamond pin to the front—and several friends were gathered in the parlor, the men smoking, while Catrina gave them some complicated Wagnerian music at the piano, a bomb was thrown in at the window. It was an awful thing, about the size of a cocoanut, quite as round, and had issuing from a hole a blue fire that burned and smoked in the most fearful manner. The women shrieked and fled, the men scattered, the servants yelled as they disappeared, while the thin old Fakin shot out at the door and never stopped running until he gained the depot, and took passage to Yonkers. Old Mr. Diedrich went down in a sitting position. The only one present who exhibited any presence of mind was Tom Slater. With a coolness and courage that cannot be overpraised, he seized the deadly bomb, and, carrying it to the rear of the house, threw it into the back-yard, where it exploded with a sickening thud that made Diedrich Von Cott's heart sink into his shoes.

After that all opposition to Tom Slater's wooing was withdrawn. A parent will do much for his daughter's happiness, and a good deal more for his own safety. The lovers were duly married, and, strange to say, no more skulls, cross bones, suspended fat men, or bombs appeared to mar the domestic felicity of the Von Cott family.

A STORY ABOUT BEARS.

CONSULT any number of boys as to their favorite animal, and nine out of ten will cast their free suffrage in favor of Bruin. There is something about the bear that fascinates a boy. The little four-year-old, climbing upon your knee, will call for a story about bears, and after hearing the thrilling recital he will get down behind a chair and act the part, to the mute amazement of his little sister.

This interest in the clumsy creature seems to be as instinctive as our horror of snakes. My earliest adventure, that had consequences of sufficient importance to procure me a paternal thrashing, and leave a life-long remembrance, came of an attempt to play bear. Surreptitiously possessing myself of a hair-rug that ordinarily graced the hall, I pulled it over my back and head and hid behind the gate, where a beautiful hawthorn hedge afforded superb concealment, and solemnly determined to "scare some one into fits." That "some one" happened to be old Uncle Shack's horse Gunpowder, so called from the difficulty experienced in getting him to go off.

Now this Uncle Shack was an American citizen of African descent, a sort of commissary attached to our family headquarters. He had become superannuated at the age of forty, and devoted the remainder of his colored existence to a light pursuit of vegetables. At the time I proposed to make his aged horse acquainted with bears, Uncle Shack was about sixty, gray-haired, blear-eyed, and with well-settled convictions, the most prominent of which appeared to be that boys, as a general thing, ought to be killed. On this occasion, having gathered an assortment of vegetables, he stood up in his crazy vehicle, such only as a negro can devise, and drove slowly to his doom. His horse had a tradition attached to him that at one time in his past life he had been a spirited animal. Wild stories were afloat of deeds on the road that were positively incredible to the observer. He was, at the time referred to, a living hat-rack, with nothing left of his former activity but an eccentric movement in his right hind leg, that came of the string-halt, and, while the animal seemed to be moving with the solemnity of a funeral, this leg continued the famous old trot of the road.

When directly opposite my ambush, I moved out, with head covered, on my hands and knees, growling in approved bear-fashion. Gunpowder at first seemed lost in amazement. He stopped abruptly, stared, and then, as I approached making hideous noises, he gave a fierce snort, and actually broke into a gallop. Uncle Shack attempted to arrest this by wild orders of "Whoa ! whoa !" and drafts upon the reins. These last were old and decayed ; in the midst of the effort they snapped, and the aged African came down in a sitting position upon his vegetables.

The fates then took command. From the gate to a bridge below the mill the road was descending. Along this I saw and heard the doomed vehicle roll and rattle. The race was not swift, but it was portentous in its noise and grave in its consequences. The wild horse of the vegetable garden, unguided, missed the wooden structure, and I saw wagon, rider, horse, and all disappear down a dreadful abyss of six feet. Then followed a silence fearful in its contrast to the late uproar. The wagon, horse, and man, so full of vigorous life and sense, seemed to drop through a hole and vanish from the earth.

With that diplomatic ability that has since distinguished me, I ran into the house, replaced the rug, and was among the first to give the alarm. Indeed, no proof could be adduced that I had been guilty of this outrage on bears and Africans, but I was subsequently thrashed on presumption.

The vehicular convenience for vegetables was fished out. The horse died soon after from over-exertion, and Uncle Shack survived the shock only twenty years. He dated from that event his decline and death, and, retiring from business, existed on the charity of the family and a detailed account of the dreadful affair.

Looked at from an intellectual point of view, Bruin can scarcely be considered a success. He lacks the keen instinct of the dog and the ponderous sagacity of the elephant. He has no sense of fun in his composition. He is as serious as an ass, and far more stupid. Numerous stories were told us in early youth touching this lack of common-sense, such, for example, as that of the man in the wilds of the West who was superintending a saw-mill. While sitting upon the log that was being sawed, and eating his frugal repast, a huge black bear suddenly bounced in and invited himself to dinner. The proprietor politely withdrew, clambering into the rafters above, while Bruin took his place upon the log and continued the meal. In a few seconds the approaching saw touched the rump of the bear, and he edged forward. It again rasped him, and he resented the indignity with a growl. The third time he turned furiously and hugged the saw. Then a contest ensued that was very lively but exceedingly brief. At the end the modest sawyer descended to find a remnant of his dinner and considerable bear-meat.

Again, we were assured that the common way of killing bears in Hardin forests was to suspend a log by a grape-vine to a bee-tree. Bruin, who is passionately fond of honey, in ascending the tree would knock the log aside with his paw. The log returning would hit and infuriate the bear, and, a contest arising between the two, would bring the poor beast to grief—for the harder he would strike the more severe would be the rebound. Not a bad fable is that to illustrate the evil which comes to the individual who creates strife in his own heart through hate, envy, malice, and all uncharitableness.

This fondness for sweets is only equalled by Bruin's taste for infant pig. He cannot resist the squeal of the young porker, and will run his stupid head into all sorts of traps baited with the living animal.

There is a certain lumpish activity about the bear that is extremely diverting. One must not count too positively, however, on his lack of dexterity. The late witty and eccentric Judge Tappan once had a realizing sense of this. He, with two or three companions, was boating on Lake Erie, near Sandusky, at an early day, when they observed a bear swimming from the mainland toward an island. The party, armed only with an axe. rowed in pursuit. As they approached their proposed prey, the Judge stood with axe in hand, intending to hit Bruin on the skull. But the animal, eyeing his enemy warily, was prepared, and as the axe descended he turned suddenly in the water, and with one swift stroke of his paw sent it flying from the grasp of his foe far into the lake. Then Bruin passed from the defensive to a vigorous attack. and began climbing into the boat To take such a passenger aboard was exceedingly unpleasant, and, armed with oars, the party used due diligence. It proved impossible to keep him out, but by quick concerted action they succeeded in passing him over into the water again. The bear returned to the charge, and was again tumbled out. In the third assault the boat was so filled with water that it capsized, and the adventurous pioneers found themselves swimming for life. Bruin was master of the situation, but stupidly declined the advantage As the party, clinging to the oars, swam away, they saw the bear seated upon the upturned boat regarding their exertions with philosophical indifference.

The common brown bear of North America is an insignificant creature ; and it remained for the grizzly bear of the Rocky Mountains to give dignity to the species. What an immense, fearful animal it is ! We owe much to the grizzly bear. He aided, in lieu of war, to lift our money-getting people to a higher level of manhood. Nothing but the discovery of gold in California could drag us from our counting-rooms, workshops, and fields. The hazardous crossing of vast deserts and trackless mountains, the fights with Indians, and. above all, the adventures with the grizzly bear, developed the manhood found. strange to say, in the combative instincts of our nature. I never meet with a Californian now but I am impressed with the presence of a stronger and larger man than the ordinary American.

An encounter with a grizzly bear is fraught with peril. The creature s strength, courage, and strange vitality, make the deadly contest nearly even between the armed man and the unarmed beast. Heaven help the hunter whose unsteady aim leaves the bear uncrippled. Before he can reload, the enemy will be upon his works. When the contest is narrowed to that pass, Daniel Boone's celebrated prayer, when the famous pioneer found himself face to face with the common brown bear, would be a waste of breath. The petition is well worth putting to record as a specimen of Western humor, if not an incident in the life of Boone. "O Lord," piously cried the fighter, in the brief pause given him previous to the deadly combat between a scalping-knife and the claws, "here's a-goin' to be one of the biggest b'ar-fights you ever did see. O Lord, ef you can't help me, for God's sake don't help the b'ar."

A friend of mine, a bold hunter from England, told me once of a scrape he found himself in, while hunting the grizzly bear of the Rocky Mountains. He came upon his prey quite unexpectedly, and man and beast stared at each other in some astonishment, not fifty yards apart. The bear exhibited no disposition of a mo iest or retiring sort, and my friend made haste to tender him a warm reception. He fired with more quickness than accuracy. The bullet from the heavy rifle tore away a portion of Bruin's ear, and, grazing the skull, stunned the brute for an instant. The hunter hastened to reload, but before he could do so the bear had regained his legs, and, although somewhat groggy, came at his enemy. My friend had time only to drop his rifle and spring into a tree, up which he clambered with an activity worthy of earlier youth. Grizzly, one of the largest, made short work of the rifle. Then he sat on his haunches and gazed stupidly at the man in the tree. As the pain of his mutilated ear increased, he grew furious, and, seizing the pine in which his enemy had taken refuge, he fairly shook it in his rage. My friend had a revolver in his belt, and, bringing this to bear, he favored Bruin with six shots. He might as well have popped his lead into an iron-clad. At every discharge the bear expressed intense disgust and renewed his assault upon the tree.

A seat upon the branches of a tree is not comfortable at any time ; but with a bear below on the watch, it may be considered exceedingly unpleasant. Hours wore slowly away, with the bear moving about, at times in full view, and again hidden by the underbrush. At last, about sunset, he took himself off, and our hunter was about to descend, when he again heard reports from his enemy. These were fierce growls of rage that issued from a gorge near by. My friend at first supposed the bear had encountered other hunters, but, as he heard no sound of guns nor other evidences of mortal combat, he resumed his seat and listened. The mysterious uproar continued, and what was s range appeared in the fact that it came from the same spot. Unarmed, and faint from hunger and fatigue, my friend remained all night clinging to his perch ; and at intervals he heard the bear growling and tearing furiously. The comical idea seized on the hunter, that Bruin had stupidly mistaken some other pine for the one that sheltered his enemy.

The night wore slowly away. The stars, glittering as stars can glitter only in those mountain regions, passed in their solemn march, while the deep forests of evergreens were full of strange noises to which the bear added through his eccentric conduct. My friend slept from time to time, and invariably dreamed of falling, to waken with a start, and find himself clinging to the branches of the pine. When a man sleeps in a tree, the muscles necessary to his safety do not relax as in an ordinary sleep ; but when through fatigue they are about to lose their tension, the sleeper is awakened by a dream. This is one of the singular little p' e-nomena we overlook while in search of larger ones. Who has not seen a mother in a railroad car or stage-coach, holding her infant when tired nature had forced sleep upon h r ? Her head will drop in sleep upon her breast, but the arms will not sleep ; and when, exhausted, the muscles are about to relax and let the child fall, the loving mother will awaken with a start and gather her babe nearer to her heart. Of the same sort is the fact so familiar to us all, that when one is about to start upon a journey early in the morning, and fixes in his mind before going to sleep the hour necessary to awaken, at that hour the sleeper will start into consciousness as if shaken by some friend. And I have often asked what part of us it is that remains awake to guard the infant or arouse the sleeper. The evidences of a spiritual life lie all about us, but, like our Saviour in the manger, seem so humble and insignificant that we magnificent creatures take no notice of them.

But to return to my friend. Day dawned at last, and he crawled down, sore, faint, and hungry. He was about to gather up the fragments of his rifle and hurry back to camp, when a fresh burst of rage from the wounded bear, and issuing from the same locality as during the night, so excited his curiosity that he determined to investigate, and therefore crept cautiously towards the gorge from whence the noise proceeded. The explanation made him laugh. Old grizzly had fallen into a log trap, such as hunters set when seeking to capture a living specimen. There was the last night's foe well secured, and my friend was mean enough to laugh in his face, while regarding curiously the wound his hastily discharged rifle had made. The left ear was torn away.

Nearly a year after this event, my friend, the assistant hero of the adventure, was passing along East Broadway, in New York, when his attention was attracted by a sickly hand-organ that made an orchestra to the show of a grizzly bear, with the usual accompaniment of a fat woman, the anacondas, a calf with two heads and an assortment of tails, and a monkey. Wishing to renew his acquaintance with an animal that had so nearly closed his career, my friend paid the necessary dime, and entered through a f. ul odor of decaying sawdust and fried sausages. To his amazement, in a huge iron cage, scarcely large enough to allow him standing room, was the grizzly bear he had marked in the mountains. He had been carried to San Francisco, and won great renown in several fights with bulls and dogs. He was now being exhib ted on the Atlantic slope to admiring thousands. My friend tried to catch the eye of his old adversary, but in vain. The creature's ill-temper seemed to survive his many fights and long confinement; for an awkward fellow, evidently from the interior, turned rather near the cage to gaze at the Corpulent Woman, then being festooned with anacondas, when old grizzly with a growl threw out his huge paw with such force, rapidity, and precision, that not only the back of the countryman's coat, but the seat of his stout pantaloons disappeared. My friend left the place in the midst of a fierce altercation between the country fellow and the showman, as to who should pay for "them clothes."

The strange acquaintance did not end with this. Years after, in a visit with some friends to the Zoölogical Gardens of Paris, the Englishman was delighted to recognize again his former foe. Old age, added to a better knowledge of the world, had not only subdued his ugly disposition, but life in Paris affected him as it does all native Americans, and rendered the beast positively luxurious. He received a bone kindly from his once deadly opponent, and, as the weather was extremely warm, he rolled into his stone trough to lie on his back, permitting the cool water to trickle over his hairy head, while he lazily gnawed at the bone. This falling from his indolent grasp, he closed his eyes and dropped off into a sleep, to dream such stuff as bears' dreams are made of.

I was once told how a bear was used to illustrate a fact in science. It was at an early day in the history of galvanism. A negro had been condemned to suffer death on the gallows for murder in Cincinnati, and some learned men announced that, for and in consideration of twenty-five cents admission, to be collected at the door, for the benefit of a hospital, experiments with the galvanic battery would be made upon the body of the miserable man. A circus tent had been procured for the purpose, and the medical savans counted largely on the profits to accrue.

The fatal day came, and with it thousands on thousands of people, men, women, and children, to witness the perpetuation of this remnant of stupid barbarism called hanging. From midnight until morn, from all the hills and valleys of Kentucky, Ohio, and Indiana, came pouring in the motley crowd of ignorant, curious humanity. The taverns, stores, streets, and alleys were crowded with people ; and when the sentence hour approached, the procession that accompanied the cart made a sensitive mind sick of the human race.

The better cultivated and more refined gathered in the huge tent to witness the scientific experiments, that promised to restore the wretched convict to life, or, failing in that, to make his dead body struggle and kick in the most exciting manner. The preparations were significant and startling. Near the centre of the sawdust ring was a table, and by it the wonderful instrument that was believed to hold the mysterious essence of life. About them were gathered in groups the medicated philosophers con-

versing in low measured tones, or walking to and fro, calmly indifferent to the gathered crowd, as great men are wont to do on
such occasions.

Hours wore away. The noon came and passed. The excitement grew intense. At last a rumor spread and reached the tent
that the sentenced man had been reprieved upon the scaffold. This
was confirmed by the returning crowd, that pushed in without
paying and packed every available space. Hisses and cries of discontent broke out, and were taken up by the motley crew of the
non-paying audience, in a high state of wrath at being disappointed
in the hanging   In the midst of the tumult Professor D——
mounted the table, and, commanding silence, said : "Ladies and
gentlemen, we regret deeply that a mistaken clemency on the
part of the Governor has robbed the gallows of its own and science
of a subject. It is impossible to return you your money, for so
many have rushed in without paying, and they would be precisely
the sort to demand the admission fee. We have determined, however, so that you may not be disappointed in your laudable curiosity to witness an execution and those wonderful exhibitions of
modern science, to purchase of Mr. Brown a bear that he has fat-
tened to kill, hang the animal here, and then proceed with our
experiments. Will this satisfy you?"

An uproarious and unanimous shout in the affirmative was the
response. The bear was sent for. But Bruin had not been consulted, and declined the engagement. The audience waited
impatiently for hours. At last a great noise of men, boys,
and dogs on the outside gave welcome note of the coming
event. The fat janitor of the Medical College, a bald-headed enthusiast in the cause of physic, appeared inside the entrance, tug-
ging at a rope that seemed to be held by some reluctant party
outside. So reluctant was this party that twice the fat janitor
disappeared, pulled back by superior force. The janitor, cheered
by the crowd, and at length assisted by stout men, pulled the animal into the arena.

To hang a bear without the animal's consent (and I never
heard of one committing suicide) is at any time difficult ; but to
hang a fat bear is almost impossible. The muscular neck is quite

as large as the head, and on this occasion Bruin was pulled up twice, and twice, assisted by his paws, he twisted his neck out of the noose and came down with a sickening thud amid loud cheers from the crowd that was rapidly passing into sympathy with the four-footed animal. The third attempt proved the charm. Bruin kicked and struggled at the end of a line as naturally as a man would have done, and at the close of twenty minutes he was pronounced a dead bear by the learned facul y in attendance.

The body was lowered with some haste and placed upon the table.

Professor D., getting on a chair, said : "Ladies and gentlemen, we have at last hanged the bear. To satisfy you, however, that he is dead, we will now proceed to amputate his tail."

Loud applause followed this announcement. It prolonged the show. Brown, the butcher, performed the surgical operation by one blow of his cleaver. The bear never moved, but the flow of blood that followed demonstrated that hanging a bear causes a congestion in the tail. The battery was applied and at the first shock the struggles were renewed. At the second discharge the efforts were more decided, and growls were added. At the third shock Bruin sat upon his haunches and gazed stupidly at the audience. The audience reciprocated the attention by still louder cheers. While this was going on, the subject of these wonderful experiments happened to get sight of the fat janitor, and, while the fourth shock was being administered, he suddenly, with a terrific growl, jumped from the table and ran after his corpulent foe. The ring, that up to this moment had been somewhat crowded, was abruptly cleared. A fair field was given the affrighted official, who fairly astonished himself at the r.te with which he carried his adipose over the ground. The entertainment was impromptu, but well regulated, and, to everybody but the janitor, extremely diverting. The two were near enough matched to allow even bets, that were freely offered and as freely taken. The janitor was impelled by fear; the bear by electricity. The janitor was short of wind; the bear short of blood, and it was difficult to say which would prove the victor.

In all such exhibitions, however, certain women are sure to

be present who mar the enjoyment by screaming at the wrong moment, and then, fainting. force people to carry them into the open air. This is to be reprehended, and the women should be rebuked. On this occasion, when the popular enjoyment was at the highest and the hated janitor—by the way, a body-snatcher—was making his third round, with the bear gaining on him, three or four inconsiderate women began screaming. The people of that day were familiar with bears and had no fear of the animal. But there was something mysteriously alarming about a bear that had been dead and was alive again. And so when the screams were heard a great panic fell upon the crowd. The effort made to escape was fearful. Over the seats, under the seats, out through the thin canvas in every direction, the multitude fled like rats from a falling house, and in the midst of the tumult the canvas came down. Out from under it the audience hurried, climbing on fences and roofs, or disappearing down streets and alleys. Among these was the persecuted janitor. At last the medicated bear, full of galvanism, appeared and set off over the common, followed by all the dogs of the country.

For many years after this strange event in Cincinnati and its vicinity, hanging was regarded with great contempt. The simple folk believed that all the condemned had to do was to sell himself to the doctors. "Then those learned chaps would knock a little lightning into the body, and set it on end as good as ever."

www.ingramcontent.com/pod-product-compliance
Lightning Source LLC
Chambersburg PA
CBHW020009030726
47500CB00002B/510